W9-BZH-832

A boyfriend thief?

"Come on, stop acting so innocently, Elizabeth," Robin said. "You deliberately stole my boyfriend."

Elizabeth was completely dumbfounded. What was Robin talking about? Stealing her boyfriend? Since when was Todd Robin's boyfriend?

Wait a minute . . . Elizabeth thought about all the clues Robin had given her and Jessica about her mystery boy: brown eyes, dark hair, a great athlete . . . first name was only one syllable. "Todd?" she whispered.

"Yes, Todd," Robin said angrily.

"But I didn't know— I thought you liked somebody else—but not—never—"

Robin laughed. "Nice try, Elizabeth. You knew Todd was the only guy I ever liked! And now you're flirting with him, trying to get him to like you more than he likes me. Well, it's not going to work, so you might as well give up."

"Give—give up?" Elizabeth stammered.

"Todd's mine," Robin said. "You're not going to steal him from me. I'm not going to give him up without a fight, and as far as I'm concerned, from now on it's war between us!"

WITHDRAWN

REDWOOD

LIBRARY
NEWPORT
R.I.
Gift of
Cassie Helms

SWEET VALLEY TWINS

The Cousin War

Written by
Jamie Suzanne

Created by
FRANCINE PASCAL

BANTAM BOOKS
NEW YORK • TORONTO • LONDON • SYDNEY • AUCKLAND

To Andrew Herbert Jacobson

RL 4, 008-012

THE COUSIN WAR
A Bantam Book / September 1995

*Sweet Valley High® and Sweet Valley Twins® are
registered trademarks of Francine Pascal*

Conceived by Francine Pascal

*Produced by Daniel Weiss Associates, Inc.
33 West 17th Street
New York, NY 10011*

Cover art by James Mathewuse

*All rights reserved.
Copyright © 1995 by Francine Pascal.
Cover art copyright © 1995 by Daniel Weiss Associates, Inc.
No part of this book may be reproduced or transmitted
in any form or by any means, electronic or mechanical,
including photocopying, recording, or by any information
storage and retrieval system, without permission in
writing from the publisher.
For information address: Bantam Books*

*If you purchased this book without a cover, you should be aware
that this book is stolen property. It was reported as "unsold and
destroyed" to the publisher and neither the author nor the publisher
has received any payment for this "stripped book."*

ISBN: 0-553-48192-4

Published simultaneously in the United States and Canada

*Bantam Books are published by Bantam Books, a division of Bantam
Doubleday Dell Publishing Group, Inc. Its trademark, consisting of the
words "Bantam Books" and the portrayal of a rooster, is Registered in the
U.S. Patent and Trademark Office and in other countries. Marca
Registrada. Bantam Books, 1540 Broadway, New York, New York 10036.*

PRINTED IN THE UNITED STATES OF AMERICA

OPM   0 9 8 7 6 5 4 3 2 1

One

◇

"I can't believe Robin's actually going to be here in two hours," Jessica Wakefield said to her family. It was Saturday morning, and the Wakefields were having brunch in the kitchen. "It feels like forever since the last time we saw her."

Jessica's favorite cousin in the world, Robin Wakefield, was coming to visit for two entire weeks, and Jessica couldn't wait. Robin was a couple of months younger than Jessica, and she lived in San Diego, several hours' drive away from the Wakefields' home in Sweet Valley, California.

"She hasn't been to Sweet Valley for at least a year," said Elizabeth, Jessica's identical twin sister. "Not since we got separate rooms, anyway." The twins had gotten their own rooms that year, when they started sixth grade.

"Who's going to have the honor of letting Robin stay in her room?" Mr. Wakefield asked. "And Steven, please pass the pepper, if you don't mind."

Steven, the twins' fourteen-year-old brother, handed the salt and pepper shakers across the kitchen table to their father. "Gee, I wish Robin could stay in *my* room," he said. "Maybe we could stay up really late and paint our nails together."

Jessica glared at him. Of course Steven had to act as if Robin's visit was no big deal. *He* didn't know anything about friendship, or what it was like to want to stay up all night talking and laughing. "She'd rather die than stay in your room," she told her brother. "As if she could even find a place to sleep, with all your junk."

"Look who's talking!" Steven laughed. "Your room's way messier than mine."

"Jessica's room is messier than anyone on the planet's," Elizabeth added, buttering her toast.

"Hey! No fair ganging up," Jessica said. Maybe her bedroom was a little disorganized, and maybe she had a hard time finding things sometimes, but that didn't mean it was *messy*. Was it her fault that she was just too busy to care about details like putting her clothes into the laundry basket? She did have a social life, after all.

"Still, you might want to clean up a bit before Robin's bus gets in," Mrs. Wakefield said. "So she can find a place to put her things."

"She can put them in my room," Elizabeth offered.

"That reminds me, Jessica—we never decided who she's going to stay with first."

"Me, of course," Jessica said, digging into her omelet.

"Why 'of course'?" Elizabeth asked.

"Because," Jessica said. "It was my idea for her to visit, wasn't it?"

Elizabeth shook her head and laughed. "No, actually, don't you remember, Jess? Mom and Dad surprised us with the news."

"Yeah, but I'd *thought* about having her visit way before they told us," Jessica declared. "And that means Robin stays in my room for the first week she's here—and in yours the second week."

Elizabeth stared at her a minute, then sighed. "OK, if you say so. It's not worth fighting over."

Jessica smiled triumphantly. She knew she might have twisted Elizabeth's arm a little bit, but Robin just had to stay in her room first. She couldn't wait to show her younger cousin around, to introduce her to all her friends at school, to point out all the cute guys and ask Robin who she thought was the best-looking.

But right now, there wasn't any doubt in Jessica's mind that the answer was Juan Valencia. Juan was an exchange student from Argentina, staying with Aaron Dallas, a sixth-grader on the soccer team with Juan. Juan's living arrangement presented a slight problem for Jessica, because Aaron was her sort-of boyfriend. Whenever there were dances or parties at Sweet Valley Middle School, she usually went with Aaron. And now there was a huge dance at school coming up, probably the hugest of the year—and she didn't want to go with Aaron. She wanted to go with Juan. Fortunately, it was a Sadie Hawkins dance, which meant the girls got to ask the boys. Jessica had the chance to ask whomever she wanted. She definitely planned on asking Juan.

She glanced across the table at her sister. Elizabeth would probably end up asking Todd Wilkins to the dance. No matter how many times Jessica pointed out that Todd was boring, and that going out with the same boy for weeks and weeks on end was boring, Elizabeth still insisted on dating Todd. Not that there was anything *that* wrong with Todd. He was even cute . . . in a boring kind of way. He just wasn't somebody Jessica would ever choose.

Then again, Jessica and Elizabeth had different opinions about most things, not just boys. The twins looked the same on the outside—each had long golden blond hair, blue-green eyes, and a dimple in her left cheek. But the similarities ended there.

Elizabeth was the more serious, studious twin. Her favorite activities included reading mystery novels and writing for *The Sweet Valley Sixers*, the sixth-grade newspaper that she had helped start. Her best friends were Amy Sutton and Maria Slater, who Jessica thought were just as boring as Todd.

Jessica, on the other hand, liked to spend time with

her fellow members of the Unicorn Club, a group made up of the prettiest and most popular girls at Sweet Valley Middle School. The Unicorns loved to talk about fashion, movie stars, and boys. Jessica considered her friends way more fun than Elizabeth's. But even if she and Elizabeth couldn't agree on a lot of things, Jessica knew that her sister would do anything in the world for her, and vice versa.

Plus, because they were identical twins, they were best friends in a close way that nobody else could really understand. Sometimes Jessica even believed that she could tell what Elizabeth was thinking.

And right now, she was probably thinking, *I wish Robin were staying in my room first instead of Jessica's!* Jessica mused with a smile.

Steven Wakefield crumpled his napkin into a ball and stuffed it underneath his plate. He hadn't finished all his waffles, but the thought of Robin's visit was making him lose his appetite. Hadn't he put up with enough, living with twin sisters? He'd dealt with pillow fights, shrieking matches, silly crushes, endless practical jokes. It was more than any human being should have to endure.

And now? Just when he thought he'd seen everything, his little cousin Robin was coming to visit. Sure, Robin was nice and everything—on her own. But put her in a house with his bratty twin sisters and what do you get? Three silly, loser girls ruining Steven's life.

I wish I could move out for a couple of weeks, he thought. But he'd already checked with his best friends—either they didn't have enough room in their houses for a two-week houseguest, or their parents didn't think it was a good idea.

So instead, I'm going to lose my mind, Steven thought, frowning at the waffles on his plate.

"What are you in such a bad mood about?" Elizabeth asked, reaching for the pitcher of orange juice.

"Guess," Steven grumbled.

"I bet he got turned down for a date tonight," Jessica said knowingly. "And he's depressed."

"No, I didn't get rejected, Einstein," Steven said.

"Well, it's only a matter of time," Jessica said, tossing back her blond hair.

Elizabeth laughed. "Jessica, don't say that! Anyway, *we're* the ones who need dates. For the Sadie Hawkins dance."

"Well, I know who *I'm* going to ask," Jessica said confidently. "And I'm not worried at all about being turned down."

"Maybe you'd better start worrying," Steven said with a sneer. "Have you looked in the mirror lately?"

"OK, kids, that's enough," Mrs. Wakefield said, breaking open a muffin. "I hope you'll make an effort to get along while Robin's staying with us."

"Oh, Elizabeth and I will be easy to get along with, as always," Jessica said, smiling at her brother. "The question is, what about Steven?"

"I'll get along all right," Steven said through clenched teeth. "No problem."

"Gate twelve," Elizabeth said, looking around the bus station. "There it is!" She and Jessica hurried across the lobby to stand by the door where the bus from San Diego would pull in. Mrs. Wakefield was waiting in the car for them.

"You know, being at the bus station makes me think," Jessica asked. "We need to go on more trips."

"That would be fun," Elizabeth said, nodding. "Where to?"

"You know where I've always, always wanted to go?" Jessica asked.

"Paris?" Elizabeth guessed.

Jessica shook her head. "Argentina."

Elizabeth laughed. "Jessica, you didn't even know where Argentina *was* until Juan came here a few weeks ago and talked about it in social studies." She pushed up the sleeves of her blue sweatshirt.

"That's not true. I just happen to know a lot more about it now, that's all," Jessica said. "And the more I know, the more I like." She leaned against the row of lockers on the wall and sighed.

Elizabeth gave Jessica a sideways look. "Do you have a crush on Juan, by any chance?"

"No way," Jessica replied, twirling a finger in her hair. "It's just that Argentina's a beautiful country, and Juan just . . . happens to be a really nice person, that's all. And an incredible soccer player."

"That's for sure," Elizabeth agreed. "Actually, I'm going to interview him for the all-sports special edition of the *Sixers*. He really helped us win the last couple of games."

Jessica's eyes lit up. "An all-sports edition? Will there be any pictures in that special edition? You know, big pictures?"

"Pictures?" Elizabeth asked innocently. "Pictures of who?"

"Of the team, of course," Jessica said quickly. "And maybe some close-ups of the star players."

Elizabeth giggled. She was just about to tease Jessica when an announcement came over the loudspeaker.

"Now arriving at gate twelve, our express from San Diego," the bus station manager's voice crackled.

"She's here!" Jessica exclaimed.

Elizabeth yanked open the door and watched as a stream of passengers stepped down off the bus. Suddenly, she spotted a tall, pretty girl with chin-length blond hair. She wore a black jean jacket, a bright striped T-shirt, and black jeans and was standing on tiptoe, peering around the crowd. "Robin! Over here!" Elizabeth called to her.

Robin waved and ran over to the twins, who threw their arms around her. "It's so good to see you guys!" Robin cried.

"I've missed you so much!" Jessica replied, hugging her tightly. "Wow, you've gotten so much taller—you're taller than me, and you're supposed to be my younger cousin. What's the deal?"

"I went through this major growth spurt last spring," Robin said. "I grew out of half my clothes!"

"You look great. We're so glad you're here," Elizabeth said. "Good thing your parents went to Europe!"

"Yeah, I know." Robin stepped back and smiled at them both. "At first I was bummed they weren't taking me with them, but then they told me I could come visit you." Her eyes sparkled. "And who needs Paris when you can go to Sweet Valley?"

"Yep, Sweet Valley is a lot more exciting than Paris," Jessica declared.

"This is going to be the best two weeks ever," Elizabeth added, picking up one of Robin's two very large duffel bags. "Do you think you brought enough clothes, though?" she teased.

Robin laughed. "Hey, you guys didn't exactly make packing any easier for me, you know. Let's see—you said something about maybe going sailing, and horseback riding, and going out to dinner, too."

"Well, we left out the most important thing of all," Jessica told her. "You *only* decided to show up during the *most* exciting time of the entire year. Wait until you hear what's going on next weekend!" She put her arm around Robin's shoulders, and the two of them started walking through the bus terminal to the parking lot on the other side.

"Jessica? Can you grab Robin's other bag?" Elizabeth called out after them.

"OK, first you have to meet all my friends Monday at school," Jessica went on as she and Robin proceeded toward the door. "And *then* . . ."

Typical Jessica, Elizabeth thought, shaking her head. *She's so caught up in talking to Robin that she forgot all about me.* Elizabeth bent down and struggled to pick up the other duffel bag. Both bags were heavy, and she tried to balance them by putting the straps around her shoulders. She had a feeling that the next two weeks would be more than just exciting—they would be exhausting, too.

But she didn't really care—Robin was in town, and they were going to have a blast!

Two

◇

"So tell us everything that's been going on in your life," Elizabeth said to Robin later that night.

"And give us all the juicy details," Jessica added. She took a brownie off the plate in the middle of the floor and leaned back against her bed.

The three girls were all set to talk and snack until at least midnight. Jessica had even cleaned her room for the occasion, shoving everything into her closet to make room for the three of them.

Robin felt incredibly relaxed and at home, hanging out at her cousins' house. She was having a great time so far.

She took a handful of cheese curls and popped one into her mouth. "I don't have any exciting news, really."

"I think she's holding out on us," Elizabeth said to Jessica. "What do you think?"

Robin laughed. "You sound like a detective. Really, my life's been very boring lately. I go to school—"

"Say no more." Jessica held up both hands, brownie crumbs dropping onto the rug. She quickly swept them under her bed. "If it's about your classes, we don't want to know."

"Jessica doesn't, anyway," Elizabeth said. "We can talk about that stuff later, since you'll be coming to classes with us."

"But what about the important stuff?" Jessica asked impatiently. "Have you been, you know, dating anyone?"

Robin blushed. "Nope."

"What? Are you serious?" Jessica demanded.

"It's not a crime, Jess," Elizabeth said, laughing.

"I'm not saying it's a crime—I just can't believe it. I mean, you're so pretty," Jessica said. "How can you not have a boyfriend?"

"Easy. There isn't anyone back in San Diego that I really like," Robin replied. "And believe me, I've looked around and considered *all* my options. From the cool guys to the nerds. There just isn't anyone who's right for me."

"Hmm." Jessica tapped her fingers against the floor. "That's not good."

Elizabeth rolled her eyes. "Jessica, you make it sound like Robin's coming down with a disease. Not having a boyfriend isn't really a big deal."

"Actually, Jessica has a point," Robin said. "In fact, I was kind of hoping I might meet someone I like while I'm here."

"That's perfect!" Jessica cried. "A vacation romance!"

"It is?" Robin asked, furrowing her brow.

"Definitely," Jessica answered, reaching for an orange soda. "Remember, I mentioned that dance at school next weekend? It's a Sadie Hawkins Dance. You pick out somebody you like, ask them to the dance—presto!" She snapped her fingers. "Instant boyfriend!"

"I don't know," Robin said hesitantly. The prospect of finding a boyfriend was exciting, but she didn't know if she could actually ask out somebody she didn't even know. She was pretty shy when it came to boys. "How will I know who to ask?"

"We can help you, if you want," Elizabeth offered. "We know everyone at school, and we'll introduce you to them. But only if you want," she added, giving Jessica a look. "Don't feel like you *have* to ask someone."

"She does too have to! Robin, it's going to be great," Jessica promised. "You can go to the dance with him on Friday, and then you'll still have a whole extra week to spend here, hanging out with him. And of course, if it doesn't work out, then boom—you're out of town in a week and you won't ever have to deal with him again!"

"Not work out?" Robin repeated, feeling a little

nervous. "What do you mean exactly?"

"She's just giving you the worst-case scenario," Elizabeth said quickly. "Right, Jessica?"

"Right," Jessica agreed. "I just didn't want Robin to feel pressured or anything."

Robin smiled and thought about it for a minute. It would be hard to ask out a total stranger, but who knows? It might be worth the effort. "I guess it'd be OK to ask somebody to the dance. But how am I going to find somebody I like in less than a week?"

"It'll be easy," Jessica assured her. "There are lots of cute guys at our school. Trust me."

"So which cute guy are you going to ask?" Robin asked, smiling.

Jessica turned pink. "Well . . ." she began.

"Are you still going out with that guy—what's his name?" Robin asked. Jessica had mentioned a sort-of boyfriend in her last few letters. Actually, her letters were all about boys, while Elizabeth's were usually full of questions for Robin, and news about her writing or her best friends.

"Aaron, and no," Jessica said. "Not really. I mean, technically, maybe, but—"

"But you want to ask somebody else?" Robin finished.

Jessica nodded eagerly. "There's this totally cute guy named Juan Valencia."

"Ha! So you admit it!" Elizabeth exclaimed triumphantly.

Jessica looked at her with wide eyes. "Of course

I admit it. I'm not someone who would keep something like this a secret, you know."

"That's funny," Elizabeth said, smiling snidely. "I could have sworn that earlier today you insisted you *didn't* have a crush on Juan."

"He's an exchange student from Argentina," Jessica told Robin, ignoring Elizabeth's comment. "And he's practically the best soccer player in the world, and he's got these gorgeous brown eyes." She sighed. "He's perfect."

"He happens to be nice, too," Elizabeth told Robin. "On top of everything else."

"He sounds great," Robin said. "I wish there were guys like that in San Diego!"

"There's no one like him anywhere in the world," Jessica said dreamily.

Robin giggled. "So when are you going to ask him? You should hurry—you wouldn't want somebody else to ask him before you do."

"Oh, I'm not worried," Jessica said confidently. "I'll probably ask him on Monday, and I know for sure that he doesn't have a date yet."

"Jess, isn't there just one little problem?" Elizabeth asked. "How's Aaron going to feel about the fact that you're asking his houseguest to the dance, instead of him?"

"Aaron?" Jessica asked, as though she'd never heard the name before.

"Your sort-of boyfriend?" Elizabeth pressed. She turned to Robin. "Aaron and Jessica have gone on at least ten dates so far this year."

"Well, that doesn't mean we're married or any-thing, you know," Jessica responded. "Besides, I'm sure Aaron will be glad that his houseguest is hav-ing a good time and making friends."

"Oh, I'm sure," Elizabeth said, smiling.

Robin giggled. "What about you, Elizabeth? Have you asked anyone yet?"

"No-o," Elizabeth said slowly. "And actually . . . I'd rather not say who I'm going to ask."

"What?" A big smile lit up Jessica's face. "Did you just say you're not sure who you're asking? Does that mean your taste in boys has improved since last week?"

Elizabeth rolled her eyes. "All it means is—well, I just . . . feel funny talking about asking boys on dates. And so I don't want to jinx it, that's all."

"Since when do you believe in jinxing things?" Robin asked. "Whenever Jessica and I start talking about superstitions and horoscopes and stuff like that, you always say you're not interested."

"What? Aren't I allowed to change at all since the last time I saw you?" Elizabeth asked.

"Now that you ask, no, you're not!" Robin said, tossing a cheese curl at Elizabeth.

Elizabeth laughed. "And I suppose you haven't gotten your hair cut once since we saw you?"

"Of course not," Robin said. "I'd never change a thing about my looks without consulting you guys first."

"Funny, those don't look like the same jeans you had on when we came to visit you," Elizabeth replied, tossing a cheese curl at Robin.

"Is it my fault I've gotten taller since then?" Robin asked, throwing it back at Elizabeth.

"Now that you mention it—yes!" Elizabeth cried, tossing a handful of cheese curls at Robin, who screamed and started throwing them back at Elizabeth.

Suddenly there was a loud pounding on the door. "Uh-oh, here come your parents," Robin whispered. "Hope I didn't get us in trouble."

"Hey, could you keep it down in there?" Steven called through the closed door. "Some of us are trying to get some sleep tonight. It's kind of hard when you guys are in there screaming like banshees. My room *is* right next door."

"Don't remind us!" Jessica cried.

"Sorry, Steven," Elizabeth said, suppressing her giggles. "We're trying to keep it down."

"Yeah, well, try harder," Steven grumbled. They heard him walk down the hall, and Elizabeth and Robin burst out laughing.

"Steven's right, you guys. Stop fooling around," Jessica said. "We have some serious work to do." She reached under her bed and pulled out a huge stack of magazines. "Leo, right?" she asked Robin.

Robin scooted closer on the floor. "Right. Now what does it say about my love life for this month?"

Jessica cleared her throat. "Prepare yourself,

Leo," she read out loud. "You may meet the guy of your dreams on a trip this month."

"It does not say that!" Robin squealed, grabbing the magazine from Jessica.

"Can I help it if I know more than Sapphira Stargazer?" Jessica asked with a shrug, and the three of them burst out laughing all over again.

Monday at school, Jessica and Elizabeth gave Robin a tour, brought her to their morning classes, and then split up for lunch. Jessica wanted Robin to meet all her friends in the Unicorn Club, and Elizabeth wanted to eat lunch with Amy Sutton.

"This is what we call the Unicorner," Jessica said, leading Robin across the lunchroom to a table in the corner, where some of her friends in the Unicorn Club were already sitting. "We meet here every day for lunch. Nobody else sits here, because they know it's our spot."

Mandy Miller looked up from her seat. "Hi! You must be the famous Robin!"

"Gee, I didn't realize I was famous," Robin said, blushing.

"Believe me, Jessica's been talking about you for weeks. Have a seat," Mandy offered, sliding her tray over on the table. "I'm Mandy, and this is Grace, and that's Lila."

"Thanks. Hi, everyone." Robin smiled and slid into the seat beside Mandy.

Jessica took a seat across from her. "So what's new with you guys?"

"We were just talking about the dance," Lila Fowler, Jessica's best friend, said. She flipped her long, brown hair over her shoulder. "For one thing, I absolutely have to go shopping this week. I don't have anything to wear to that dance."

Jessica shook her head. "Lila, you only have the biggest wardrobe of anyone. In fact, you probably have more clothes than the rest of the sixth grade combined." Lila's father was a wealthy business-man, and she lived in a mansion with a huge swim-ming pool, round-the-clock maid service, and even a chauffeur and a limousine.

Lila grinned. "Well, this is a very important dance, you know. I want just the right thing."

"Did you already ask Jake to go with you?" Mandy asked.

Lila nodded. Jake Hamilton was Lila's sort-of boyfriend. They'd gone to a few dances together. "He said yes, of course."

"What other answer is there?" Jessica said with a shrug.

"What about you, Jessica?" Lila asked, a gleam in her eye. "Don't tell me you still haven't asked anyone."

Jessica shook her head. It was just like Lila to be competitive with her about the dance. "No, but don't worry—I will."

Jessica glanced to where Juan was sitting, a few tables away. She'd show Lila. She was only going to the dance with the cutest boy in the entire school. She just had to get up the nerve to ask him, that was all. She'd do it. She just wasn't sure when. She decided to turn everyone's attention to Robin's dilemma. "Anyway, the big news is that Robin's going to the dance, too, and she needs to find a date, fast."

"Hmm." Mandy raised an eyebrow. "You need a date, huh? Have you picked anyone out yet?" She surveyed the lunchroom. "I think I see a few candidates."

Robin laughed. "Maybe you can ask somebody *for* me. You know, be my agent, or social secretary or whatever."

"Sorry." Mandy shrugged. "I have a hard enough time handling my own social life. It's a twenty-four-hour job, you know."

"Don't worry about asking somebody, Robin," Lila said. "Who's going to say no to you? You'll find a date. No problem."

"Hey, that reminds me," Grace said. "A bunch of us were talking in science class this morning about going bowling this afternoon."

"Bowling?" Lila said, looking as if Grace had just said they were all going to jump off a cliff that afternoon. "You mean, at a bowling alley?"

"No, we're going to try to knock people over with bowling balls at the mall," Mandy said, rolling her eyes. "Come on, Lila, the Bowl-o-rama is a great place. It's so tacky there that it's almost cool. Anyway, bowling's fun."

"Yeah," Jessica agreed. "My family goes all the

time." Usually she had to deal with Steven's bragging about how much higher his score was than hers. It would be nice to go with friends. "So who's going this afternoon?"

"Everyone, I think," Grace said. "You and Robin want to come?"

Jessica nodded, her mind whirling. *Everyone— maybe that means Juan!* "We have to go," she said, turning to Robin. "This is the perfect opportunity for you to meet a boy to ask to the dance."

"Yeah, see who looks the best in those bowling shoes with the little numbers on the back," Mandy advised.

"And see who wears the least polyester," Lila said. "Anyone who brings their own bowling ball is definitely out!"

Robin giggled. "Don't worry, I have *some* standards. But this could be embarrassing—I've only gone bowling a couple of times before."

"Well, you can't be a worse bowler than me," Mandy said. "Last time I tried to roll the bowl down the lane, it went rolling *backwards,* onto my dad's foot."

"No way," Jessica said, laughing. "Well, hopefully, we'll all do better than that. In more ways than one." She glanced over at Juan and Aaron's table again. Everyone was laughing at Aaron, who was trying to balance a spoon on his nose.

Juan would never do anything as goofy as that, Jessica thought, gazing at him. He looked so cute in his World Cup T-shirt, with his dark-brown hair tucked behind his ears.

Suddenly, Jessica just had to make sure Juan would be at the bowling alley that afternoon. "Come on, Robin—I want to introduce you to some more people," she said, standing up.

"Who?" Robin asked.

"You'll see," Jessica promised as she guided Robin to the table where Juan and Aaron were sitting. "Someone very important," she added in a whisper.

Jessica didn't normally think of herself as shy, but as she and Robin approached the table, her heart was fluttering in her chest. "Hi, you guys."

"Hello, Jessica," Juan said, smiling warmly.

"Hi, Juan," Jessica said softly, feeling as though she might faint. He looked so happy to see her, and she loved the way he pronounced her name, as if it started with an "h" instead of a "j." She decided to ask her French teacher if she could start taking Spanish instead.

"Hey, Jessica," Aaron said. "What's up?"

Jessica smiled and stared at Juan. "Nothing. I mean—I wanted you to meet my cousin, Robin. Robin, this is Juan Valencia." She felt her heart beat extra-hard as she said the name. "And Aaron Dallas," she added. His name wasn't nearly as much fun to pronounce.

"Hi," Aaron said loudly, nodding at Robin.

Juan stood up and held out his hand, which Robin shook, looking awkward. "I am very pleased to know you," Juan said.

Talk about good manners, Jessica thought, her face growing warm. Everything Juan did was so cool. He was so polite and thoughtful, he seemed about five years older than Aaron. Of course, he was probably only being so polite because Robin was *her* cousin.

"It's nice to meet you, too," Robin said.

"So are you guys going bowling this afternoon?" Aaron asked.

"Yes, will you be at the Bowl-o-drama?" Juan asked.

Robin laughed. "That's Bowl-o-*rama*," she said to Juan, who shrugged and grinned at her.

"Isn't that funny. That's what I came over to ask *you*," Jessica said, staring at Juan.

"Yeah, we're going," Aaron answered, sounding a little irritated.

"Yes. I think I will look like a . . . how do you say . . . nerd, but I will try," Juan said.

Like a nerd? Never! Jessica wanted to say. Unless nerds were going to start being incredibly gorgeous, with deep-brown eyes, light-brown skin, and beautiful smiles. *Not likely.* The first bell rang, indicating the end of lunch period. "OK, so we'll see you later, then," Jessica told Juan and Aaron.

"Will you go, too?" Juan asked Robin just before she and Jessica walked away.

"Oh, sure. See you!" Robin called over her shoulder. She tugged at Jessica's sleeve as they walked out of the cafeteria. "He's as cute as you said!"

"No, he's not," Jessica said, shaking her head. "He's even *cuter!*"

Maybe I can ask him to the dance this afternoon, at the bowling alley, she told herself. One way or another, she had to go to the dance with him. No matter what!

Three

◇

Elizabeth was sitting in front of the computer in the *Sixers* office Monday afternoon when suddenly the screen went blank. She gasped and pressed a few buttons on the keyboard, trying to reboot the system. Nothing happened.

I just lost the article I wrote, she realized. She crawled underneath the desk and flicked the on-off switch, then looked up at the screen. Nothing! *I might have just lost the entire newspaper!* Elizabeth thought in a panic, as she sank back into her chair. The special all-sports edition of the *Sixers* was supposed to be done by the end of the week—and now she had absolutely nothing! She was about to scream from frustration when the door opened and Todd Wilkins walked into the office.

"Hi, Elizabeth," he said, smiling. "What's up?

Or should I say what's wrong? You look upset."

"It's this stupid computer!" Elizabeth cried. "I think the hard drive just crashed."

"No way." Todd set his books on top of the file cabinet by the door and hurried to her side. "Are you sure? How can you tell?"

"I can't get anything to come up on the screen," Elizabeth said. "The hard drive probably crashed." She put her head in her hands. "My life is ruined."

"I'm sorry," Todd said meekly.

"It's OK. I mean, it's not your fault." Elizabeth looked up at Todd with a faint smile.

"So, um, does this mean you can't go bowling this afternoon with everyone?" Todd asked, fiddling with the pencils in the cup on the desk.

Elizabeth sighed. "I'm not going bowling or anywhere else."

"Maybe you should just leave this until tomorrow," Todd suggested. "Take your mind off it. Have some fun. Then—"

"I wish I could, but I can't," Elizabeth said miserably. "If I don't start putting this issue back together, it'll never be finished on time."

"But you can't do anything now—the computer isn't working," Todd pointed out.

"Mr. Bowman is supposed to show up soon, and I'll need to get his permission to call a customer-service person or technician or whatever," Elizabeth said, pacing nervously. Mr. Bowman was the *Sixers* faculty supervisor, as well as Elizabeth's

English teacher. She turned around to look at Todd. "I'm sorry I can't come—I was really planning on it, you know."

"Oh, well. That's OK," Todd said. "I'd better take off so that I can catch up with everyone, I guess."

Elizabeth sighed. "Have fun."

"I'll see if we can bring you a souvenir bowling pin or something," Todd offered. He headed for the door, then stopped and turned around. "Isn't there something you wanted to ask me?"

"Ask you?" Elizabeth repeated.

"Yeah. Something about . . . this weekend, maybe?" Todd prompted.

"This weekend?" She remembered vaguely that there *was* something going on that weekend, but she couldn't think what it was just then. Then she snapped her fingers. "Oh, actually, there is something I want to ask you. You know my cousin's visiting, right?"

Todd nodded. "Robin. You've told me all about her."

"Well, she's going bowling with everyone today, and I told her I'd hang out with her—only now I can't. Would you mind looking after her a little bit?" Elizabeth asked.

"Sure," Todd said. "But isn't Jessica going to be there?"

"In a manner of speaking," Elizabeth said dryly. "Jessica's kind of wrapped up in her love life right now, so even though she'll be at the bowling alley, she won't *be there* be there. Know what I mean?"

"I think so," Todd said, looking confused.

"Just look out for Robin—make sure she's having a good time, OK? She doesn't really know anybody besides me and Jessica," Elizabeth said.

Todd nodded and picked up his books from the top of the file cabinet. "Got it. No problem. I'll see you later, OK? And don't stress out about the computer."

"Thanks," Elizabeth said, waving at Todd as he left the office. She sat back down at the computer and sighed. At least she could count on Todd. True, sometimes he acted a little silly and played stupid jokes on her and her friends, but basically he was a really great guy. He'd make an extra effort to be nice to Robin—Elizabeth was sure of it.

"Now if only I knew how to repair a hard drive," she said, frowning at the blank computer screen. "S.O.S.," she typed, but no words appeared on the screen. "Somebody help me!"

Robin finished tying the laces on her purple-and-yellow size-six bowling shoes and sat up. She looked around the Bowl-o-rama, wondering where Jessica had disappeared to. The Bowl-o-rama looked as though it hadn't been renovated one bit in the last twenty-five years. There were swirling yellow-and-orange shag rugs on the floor and a snack bar with green chrome stools.

"Isn't this place great?" Mandy asked, adjusting her shoelaces. She was wearing a blue shirt from a bowling league that said "Frank's Furnace Repair" on the back.

"A little tacky, but great," Robin said, smiling up at her. "I like your shirt."

"Thanks," Mandy said. "Hey, have you seen Jessica around? I need to ask her something."

"No, I haven't— Wait, there she is." Robin pointed over to lane three, where Jessica was talking to Juan. She had to admit—her cousin had really good taste. Juan had to be one of the cutest boys in Sweet Valley—he had the nicest dark brown eyes. Jessica was laughing, and Juan seemed to be having fun, too.

"Why am I not surprised she ditched us for him?" Mandy asked. "But Juan and Jessica do look cute together, I'll give her that much."

"OK, Robin, your turn!" Grace said cheerfully, walking back to take her seat after knocking down nine pins.

"I have a feeling I'm about to embarrass myself in a major way," Robin confessed to Mandy before walking up onto the wood lane.

"Don't worry—I'm after you, and you'll look like a professional compared to me," Mandy told her.

Robin walked up and held her hands over the air blower. She didn't really know why she was doing that, only the boy in the adjoining lane had just done the same thing, so she figured she was supposed to. She stared at the rack of bowling balls in front of her. How was she going to pick one? She stuck her fingers into a few of them, but they were too big for her.

"Want some help?"

Robin looked up. The boy in the lane next to hers was standing there, smiling at her. He was really cute, tall, with brown eyes, and dark hair—and he was actually talking to *her*. Robin smiled faintly. "Yeah. Do you think you could take my turn for me?"

He laughed. "Probably not, but maybe I can help you pick out a ball." He set his down, and started sorting through the balls in the rack. "Here, try this one." He held a green ball out to Robin.

She slipped her fingers and thumb into the holes. "This fits pretty well. Thanks!"

"No problem." He turned around and went back to assume the starting position. Robin watched as he coolly and casually walked up to the line and quickly released the ball. It rolled smoothly down the center of the lane, then knocked all ten pins over in one fell swoop.

"Yes!" He pumped his fist in the air.

Robin grinned at him. On top of being cute and nice, he was a great athlete, too. *Maybe Jessica's prediction was right. Maybe I will meet the boy of my dreams in Sweet Valley!* she thought excitedly. She picked up a bowling ball and tried to imitate his technique, strolling up to the line and dropping the bowling ball.

Only, hers rolled at about one-thousandth the speed his had. Within seconds, it rolled into the gutter. Robin went back to her seat and sat down before the ball had even made it to the end of the lane, too embarrassed to look the cute boy in the eye. "Told you I'd be bad," she said to Mandy with a laugh. "See if you can top *that*."

"Watch this," Mandy said confidently, striding up to pick up a bowling ball. She bent down and rolled it between her legs. It went in a straight line and knocked down half the pins. She turned around and shrugged. "Oh, well. Guess I'm better than I thought."

"Guess so," Robin said, laughing. She didn't like bowling all that much, but little by little she was getting over her embarrassment and looking forward to her next turn. After all, if there were the same number of bowlers on the adjoining lane, then she'd be up at the same time the cute boy was again. She wondered if Jessica knew him. Maybe later she could get Jessica to introduce the two of them.

When it was her turn, Robin went up to the lane, picking the green ball off the rack. She glanced over at the boy, who was getting ready to take his next turn, and smiled. He smiled back, then threw another perfect ball, knocking down all the pins.

"Another strike—wow! Congratulations!" Robin told him. "You're an amazing bowler!"

"Thanks," he said, smiling. "You could roll a strike, too, once you got the hang of it. Here, let me show you something." He stepped closer to Robin. "If you put your fingers in like this, then you should start letting go right about here. Let the ball just roll off your fingers, but give it some muscle from your arm, too."

Robin's heart started beating faster. He was standing so close to her, and he was even cuter than she'd thought. She cleared her throat and tried to compose herself. "OK, thanks. I'll try that," she said. She tossed the ball with a little more force this time, and it didn't go right into the gutter. Instead, it veered off to the right, knocking down three pins.

"Oops!" Robin blushed. "Not exactly a strike."

"It was a good try," the cute boy assured her. "Next time, just make sure your arm is straight, and you'll do even better."

Robin nodded. "Thanks for the advice!"

"You're welcome. Hey, are you thirsty? I was just about to go get a Coke—do you want anything?" he asked.

Robin felt as if she had just been knocked over like one of the bowling pins. "A—a Coke?" she stammered.

"Sure," the cute boy said. "Unless you like Sprite or something."

"Oh—um, Coke would be great," she replied, a little breathlessly.

"OK. Be right back," he said, smiling at her. "Oh, do you want something to eat—a candy bar, or some Jujubes?"

"Well . . . I love Jujubes—but well, no, I think just the Coke will be fine. Thanks!" Robin said. She didn't want to impose and ask for too much—after all, he was offering to pay for it.

"You're welcome. By the way, my name is—"

"Wilkins, I thought you were getting us Cokes!" a boy on his team called out.

"I'll be right back," he said quickly, and strode through the seats clustered around the scoring table over to the snack bar.

Robin stared after him. She couldn't believe it. Her first day hanging out with the crowd from a school she didn't even really go to, and she'd already found a boy she wanted to ask to the dance! And what was even better, he seemed to like her, too.

This is perfect! she thought. *I can't wait to tell Jessica and Elizabeth!*

"So what do you think? Am I getting better?" Jessica smiled at Juan and perched on the edge of the scorer's table.

Juan didn't look up right away—he was staring over at another lane, watching somebody else bowl.

"Juan, you missed my turn." Jessica tapped him on the shoulder.

"What? Oh, I am sorry," Juan said, turning and smiling at her. "How did you do?"

"I knocked down six. That's pretty good, isn't it?" Jessica asked, tossing her hair. "I mean, it's nothing compared to you. You're a total star bowler."

"I don't know. Todd over there looks like he is doing very much better than me," Juan said, marking Jessica's score on the screen. "But you are improving, very much. Look at this." He pointed to Jessica's score, and she leaned over his shoulder.

"I'm catching up to you!" she said excitedly.

"Yes. I am getting worried," Juan said, standing up to take his turn.

"No, you're not," Jessica said, laughing.

"Oh, yes. I may be beaten by the great Jessica, bowling queen of California." Juan smiled and stepped up into the lane.

He called me great! Jessica thought happily. Normally she would have frowned at anyone calling her a "bowling queen," but everything Juan said was so adorable, with his accent. He was even nice enough to pretend she had a fighting chance in this game, when she was forty-five points behind. She sighed. Juan was totally amazing.

"Hey, you want some chips?" Aaron came up from behind her, crunching a potato chip in his mouth.

Jessica gave the bag of chips he held out a brief glance, then turned away. "No, thanks," she replied. "I'm too busy to eat."

"Busy? You're just standing here," Aaron commented.

"I'm watching Juan!" she told him. Was he blind? There *was* another bowler in their lane. "Look—he got a strike! Way to go, Juan!" She jumped up and down, cheering.

Aaron frowned, then went up to take his turn after Juan.

"That was incredible," Jessica told Juan when he came back to stand beside her.

"It was luck, I think," Juan said, shrugging. Then he turned to look back over at lane six. *Why is he watching Todd when he could be watching me?* Jessica wondered. What was so interesting about watching another guy bowl? Especially Todd, Mr. Boring himself. "Don't tell me you're trying to pick up pointers from Todd?" she asked.

"Pointers?" Juan wrinkled his brow.

"Um . . . you know, if you watch him, you'll learn something," Jessica explained.

"Right." Juan nodded, and Jessica followed his gaze. Todd wasn't bowling anymore, but Robin was. Why was Juan staring at her cousin? Suddenly, Jessica felt all the color drain from her face. Was Juan checking Robin out?

Jessica took a deep breath, trying to clear her head. *Don't get carried away—Robin just happens to be over there next to Todd, that's all,* she told herself. And it wasn't as if Robin would fall for Juan, either—she knew that Jessica liked him.

Jessica flashed her brightest smile at Juan. "So how do you like Sweet Valley so far?"

Juan nodded, turning back to her. "I like it very much."

Jessica played with the ends of her hair. "Has Aaron been showing you all the cool places to go?"

she asked. "Because if he hasn't, I could give you a personal tour. I'll show you all my favorite places."

Aaron walked back to Juan and Jessica, and cleared his throat. "Actually, I think I've shown Juan just about everything there is in town."

Jessica's face fell. "You have?"

"Yes. Aaron is a very good host," Juan said.

"Well . . . have you been to Casey's yet?" Jessica asked. Casey's ice cream parlor, at the mall, was a major hangout for Jessica and her friends.

"Duh," Aaron said. "Only about ten times."

Jessica frowned at him. Why did he have to make everything so difficult? She was only trying to get to know Juan. OK, so maybe she and Aaron had been kind of an item, but he'd never acted jealous when she paid attention to another boy before. She decided it was time to make a dramatic exit—if only to the bathroom to put on a fresh coat of lip gloss. "I'll be right back," she said to Juan, ignoring Aaron.

"OK, but hurry," Juan told her.

He wants me to hurry! she thought. That meant he was going to miss her.

"Yeah, hurry up. You still have one more frame to bowl," Aaron told her, shoving another potato chip into his mouth.

Jessica glared at him, then turned to walk away. Typical Aaron. He was about as romantic as a cactus. Juan, on the other hand . . . he was romance personified. And pretty soon, she was going to be *his* girlfriend. She couldn't wait.

Four

"Well, at least *I* never knocked down a pin in someone else's lane," Mandy said. "Not today, anyway."

Robin laughed. "That *was* pretty funny, wasn't it?"

"That guy's still glad you knocked down his last pin," Mandy said. "I think he actually won."

"I bet you couldn't knock down the last pin in another lane if you tried," Robin teased Mandy. "It takes an incredible amount of skill."

"Uh-huh." Mandy laughed.

"I think it's something about Sweet Valley that makes me lose my touch. You should see how good I am at home. Back in San Diego, I've even won trophies," Robin joked.

"Oh, I'm sure," Mandy said, jabbing Robin playfully in the ribs. "And what do they say—lowest score ever recorded?"

Robin giggled. She was having a great time hanging out at the Bowl-o-rama except for the bowling part. Instead of getting better at her bowling during the afternoon, she'd actually gotten worse. It was all because of that boy in the next lane—whenever she got up to bowl next to him, her knees practically started knocking together and she turned into a total wreck.

He was really nice and funny about it, telling her it was no big deal and giving her advice, even though it obviously wasn't working at all. That was how she knew he was a really nice person—he didn't care whether she looked dorky and uncoordinated or not. He still talked to her and tried to help her out.

The only problem is I still have no idea who he is! She knew she could ask Mandy or Grace, but for some reason she just felt shy. Definitely too shy to ask *him* what his name was! Then she remembered the dance on Friday. She didn't have any time to be shy. If she wanted to ask this guy, she'd have to start working on it soon.

Robin glanced around the Bowl-o-rama for Jessica—her cousin always had great guy advice. But Jessica wasn't with Juan, where she'd been all afternoon. Then Robin spotted the boy she wanted to meet, standing at the shoe-rental counter all by himself. *It's now or never,* she told herself, taking a deep breath and walking over to the counter.

"I'd like to return these," she said, sliding her bowling shoes to the girl behind the desk. Then she turned as casually as she could toward him, even though her pulse was beating double-time. "Hi. You know, I just realized that we, uh, never officially met. My name's Robin," she said nervously.

"I know," he replied, smiling.

Robin felt her heart leap. He already knew who she was? He must have been asking his friends about her!

"I'm Todd Wilkins," he continued, rolling down the sleeves of his shirt. "It's nice to meet you."

"You too!" Robin said eagerly. *Incredibly nice, in fact.* "Thanks for trying to help me, even though I'm a pathetic excuse for a bowler."

Todd laughed. "No problem. You were getting better for a while there."

Until you started talking to me, Robin thought. "Well, I don't know about that. Anyway, it was really nice. I don't live here, so . . . well, it was just cool that you talked to me and stuff. I'm visiting my cousins—you probably know them. Jessica and Elizabeth Wakefield?" Robin asked.

"Oh, yeah. I know them pretty well, actually," Todd said, his eyes sparkling.

"Aren't they the greatest?" Robin asked. "Although right now I don't see Jessica anywhere, and I have no idea how we're getting home."

"There she is," Todd said, pointing behind Robin, to where Jessica was walking out of the bathroom.

"Oh, OK. Well, I'd better grab her. Maybe I'll see you at school tomorrow?" Robin said.

"Sure thing," Todd said. "Bye!"

He turned to join his friends over by the snack bar, and Robin let out a loud sigh. No doubt about it. She'd found the love of her life, just as Jessica had predicted Saturday night, when they were talking about horoscopes. And he seemed to like her, too. Now all she had to do was ask him to the Sadie Hawkins dance before anyone else did!

Her heart raced with anxiety. *What if he already has a date?* she thought for a second. *Or a girlfriend?* Then she told herself she was only being silly. If he had a girlfriend, she would have been with him all afternoon. No, it was obvious that he wasn't dating anyone. *At least not yet*, Robin thought, as she hurried over to Jessica. With any luck, he would be soon!

"I definitely want a new dress for the dance. Maybe tomorrow after school we can go to the mall and look at clothes!" Jessica said excitedly that night at dinner.

"Oh, goody," Steven said, rolling his eyes. "I'm so excited, I can't stand it."

"No, you're so grumpy, we can't stand it," Jessica retorted, passing Steven the large wooden salad bowl. "Here, have some more salad. Leafy green vegetables are good for people in bad moods."

"Yeah, make sure you take a huge helping," Elizabeth told him, and Robin laughed.

"Suddenly, I'm not hungry anymore." Steven set

his fork down on his plate. Having three girls in the house was even worse than he'd imagined. Robin had only been there for two days and he'd already suffered through countless discussions of boys, clothes, and shopping trips. He hadn't been able to sleep, because they'd stayed up late shrieking and giggling about Johnny Buck, their favorite singer, and who knew what else. His house had been taken over by girls. "Hey, Dad, did you talk to that guy at work about getting some tickets to the Lakers games?" he asked.

Mr. Wakefield nodded. "It's going to be pretty impossible. I wouldn't count on it if I were you. We can always watch the game on TV tomorrow night."

"Not on the big TV!" Jessica warned. "There's a great made-for-TV movie on tomorrow called *Passion in Paradise*. It's about falling in love on some gorgeous beach somewhere."

"The Bahamas, to be exact," Elizabeth added. "And it's not just a love story—it's a murder mystery, too."

Steven rolled his eyes. "You can tape it."

"No, you can tape the game," Jessica said.

"You can't *tape* sports," Steven replied, shaking his head. "I'll find out who won before I get to see the game!"

"Well, deal with it," Jessica said. "Robin's our guest, and *she* wants to watch the movie."

Steven groaned. This was definitely an invasion. From the planet of teenyboppers. In a couple of hours, they'd be talking and shrieking all over again, just like last night and the night before. "Mom, I'm going to sleep on the couch tonight, OK?" he announced.

"What's the matter—is your room so messy that you can't find your bed?" Jessica said, teasing him.

"No—you're so loud that I can't sleep!" Steven barked.

"Yes, you girls are going to have to keep it down," Mrs. Wakefield said. "I know you have to be tired after staying up late the past two nights."

"I don't feel tired at all," Elizabeth said with a shrug.

"Neither do I," Robin added.

"Well, good for you," Steven grumbled. "All I can say is *I'm* exhausted."

"Hey, it's not our fault you have insomnia," Jessica said. "Maybe you're really worried about something. Like finding a date this weekend." She and Robin giggled.

Steven threw his napkin down on the table. "That's it—I'm out of here!" He stood up and started to walk out of the dining room.

"Steven, come back," Mrs. Wakefield said. "The girls will promise to be nicer from now on. Won't you, girls?"

"Oh, sure," Elizabeth said. "We're sorry, Steven."

"Just not as sorry as your love life," Jessica muttered. The three girls started laughing again.

Throwing the girls one last glare, Steven stomped into the living room, flopped onto the couch, and flicked on the TV.

Twelve more days of this. It seemed like an eternity.

"I thought your parents were never going to let us go," Robin said wearily as she, Jessica, and Elizabeth went into Elizabeth's room and closed the door behind them. "Do you guys have to do the dishes every night?"

"No, just every other night," Jessica replied, sinking onto Elizabeth's bed and fluffing a pillow behind her.

Elizabeth sat in the chair at her desk. "Actually, it rotates between me, Steven, and Jessica," she said. Only, half the time she ended up taking over Jessica's night because Jessica had something else she wanted to do, like watch a movie on TV or talk to Lila on the phone. Her twin was legendary at getting out of chores. But Elizabeth didn't mind helping out, even if Jessica could be a little on the lazy side. "Don't you have to do stuff at home?" she asked Robin.

Robin nodded. "Unless I can find a way to get out of it!"

"Maybe you guys should trade ideas," Elizabeth suggested with a smile. "A hundred and one ways to get out of chores. I can see it now—it'll be a huge best-seller."

"Only if you write it," Jessica said, grinning.

"Yeah, you're the best writer," Robin said. She

gave Elizabeth a sympathetic look. "Too bad the computer ate your article today."

"Ugh. Don't remind me. I have to rewrite the whole thing," Elizabeth said, shaking her head. "But let's not talk about that. I didn't get a chance to ask you guys yet—how did the bowling go?"

"Great," Robin said breathlessly.

"Great," Jessica sighed at exactly the same time.

Elizabeth grinned. "Who wants to go first?"

"I will!" Robin said excitedly. "Elizabeth, going bowling today changed my life."

Elizabeth raised her eyebrows. "What happened? Did you discover you wanted to bowl in the Olympics or something?"

Robin shook her head. "I discovered something *much* more important than that. It's just like you said, Jessica. I found him."

"Him? Him who?" Jessica asked.

Elizabeth scooted her chair closer to Robin. "Are you saying you found a date for the dance?"

"Not just a date," Robin said dramatically. "The guy of my dreams. The one I've been waiting for forever. The—"

"*Who?*" Jessica demanded.

"Jessica, you sound like a police detective!" Elizabeth said with a laugh. "Maybe she just doesn't want to tell us."

Robin smiled. "Right. I'm following Elizabeth's example—I don't want to jinx it, so I'm going to keep it a secret for now."

Jessica frowned. "I hate secrets. What's the big deal about telling us? It's not like *we'd* tell anyone."

"What is this, twenty questions?" Robin asked. "I just agree with Elizabeth that sometimes it's better to keep things a secret—you know, until you're sure they're going to work out."

"Well, I can't argue with that, since I'm the one who said it first," Elizabeth said. "But maybe you could give us a *clue*."

"Yeah, and make it a big one," Jessica urged.

"Well . . ." Robin hesitated. "I don't know. I guess that would be OK. Maybe I could tell you what he looks like."

"Yes!" Jessica exclaimed. "Just tell us something, so we can start guessing who it is."

Robin wrinkled her nose. "Guessing? Maybe I shouldn't say anything. I mean, this is so embarrassing."

"Robin!" Jessica cried.

"You can't keep us in suspense like this!" Elizabeth protested just as loudly.

"All right, already! This is all I'm going to say for now. He has gorgeous brown eyes . . . really gorgeous. And he's a great athlete," Robin said.

"He sounds wonderful," Elizabeth mused. "Doesn't he, Jess?"

Jessica was frowning. "Um—yeah. Wonderful. I wonder who it is."

"Actually, that's my favorite type," Elizabeth went on, thinking about Todd. She'd have to give him a call later. She wished more than anything that she could have spent the afternoon bowling with him and the gang instead of with the computer-repair technician.

"Really?" Robin asked eagerly.

Elizabeth nodded and felt her face turn a little pink. "Not that I have a type or anything."

"Oh, of course not," Robin said, poking her playfully on the knee.

"But there is one boy who—"

"Hey!" Steven yelled, interrupting Elizabeth. He pounded on the bedroom door. "I'm trying to study, and Mom says you guys are supposed to be, too."

"What are you, our study hall supervisor?" Jessica retorted when Steven opened the door a crack and poked his head in.

"How can you guys make so much noise just *talking*?" he asked, looking genuinely puzzled.

"It's called an interesting conversation," Jessica said. "Not that you'd know what that is—"

"And this is called a boring conversation," Steven said. "If you guys aren't going to be quiet, I'll just have to turn up my music to drown you out." He closed the door, and seconds later, before Elizabeth could say anything else to Robin, the latest Grit Dirt CD started blaring through Steven's speakers on the other side of the wall. The lamp on Elizabeth's desk rattled to the bass beat.

"What were you saying before we were so rudely interrupted?" Robin asked Elizabeth, almost yelling. "Something about a boy?"

"Oh, I was just going to tell you about Todd," Elizabeth said.

"What?" Robin cried, as Steven turned the music up even louder. "What did you say? I can't hear you!"

"Never mind!" Elizabeth yelled back. "I'll tell you later!" It was pointless trying to talk now, thanks to Steven!

Jessica was lying on Elizabeth's bed, staring at the ceiling and trying to block out the loud music coming from Steven's room. She couldn't believe what she'd just heard her cousin say. "Gorgeous dark brown eyes . . . and a great athlete." That could only mean one person. One person named Juan Valencia. *Her* date for the Sadie Hawkins dance.

What was Robin talking about? Did she seriously think she could like Juan, and that was that? She knew that Jessica liked him. So what about friendship, loyalty . . . what about family? Hadn't she ever seen one of those emotional TV movies about families sticking together, no matter what?

Jessica tried to focus on what Robin had said, although it was hard to think with Steven's music blaring so loudly and Robin and Elizabeth shouting at each other. Maybe Robin wasn't talking about Juan. Maybe she had meant somebody else.

But Jessica certainly hadn't noticed any other great athlete with gorgeous brown eyes walking around Sweet Valley Middle School—and she had definitely looked! If Robin did really like Juan, what was Jessica going to do about it? She couldn't just stand there and watch her cousin waltz off with the cutest boy in town.

When the time comes, I'll think of something, she decided. *I always do.*

But besides asking Juan to have his handsome, slightly older brother fly in from Argentina in time for the dance, she didn't know what that would be.

Five

◇

Juan took his seat in homeroom on Tuesday morning, put his books on his desk, and leaned back in his chair to watch the doorway. *Come on*, he thought to himself. *Where is she?*

Just as he was about to wonder whether she'd called in sick, the girl he was waiting for walked into the room. He smiled at her, admiring her soft, short blond hair, her beautiful green eyes . . . He loved the tiny freckles that were sprinkled across her nose. When he'd first met her in the cafeteria, he'd thought right away that the two of them would make a good couple, even when she teased him about mispronouncing a word. Bowl-o-rama. That was one English word he'd remember forever.

Then, when he watched her at the Bowl-o-rama, he was sure he liked her. In fact, he thought she was the prettiest girl he'd ever met.

Finally, she walked through the door. "Hi, Robin," he said, as she passed him on her way to her seat in the back of the room.

"Hi, Juan," she said, smiling at him. "How's it going?"

Juan smiled back. She was even nice, on top of being beautiful. Her whole face lit up when she smiled. *Robin*, he thought. *Even her name is pretty.* "It's going great," he told her. "And how are you?"

Jessica had come into the room behind Robin, and she rushed over to her and Juan. "Good morning, Juan," she said cheerfully, slipping out of her bright-purple jacket. "I can't believe how late we are! What's up?"

"Not too much," Juan said with a shrug. He could have focused all his attention on Robin, but he knew that wasn't polite, especially since Jessica always made a point of being friendly to him. He pulled his eyes away from Robin and looked at Jessica. "What is up with you?"

"I just love the way you say that," Jessica said. "What is up. It sounds so . . . foreign."

Robin hit her lightly on the arm. "His first language *is* Spanish, dummy."

"I know," Jessica said. "And I think, considering that, you've done an incredible job learning English. I mean, you practically speak it as well as us."

"Thank you," Juan said. "Actually, we study English in school. It is not so new to me."

"Still," Jessica said, shaking her head. "I know if I had to go to a foreign country, speak a whole new language, go to school—I couldn't do it as well as you."

"Sure you could, Jessica," Robin said. "You learn really quick how to adjust. I lived in France for a year," she explained to Juan. "My dad was transferred there."

"Really? That is incredible." Juan nodded appreciatively. So he and Robin had both spent time in foreign countries. As far as he was concerned, that was just more evidence that the two of them belonged together. They'd just met, and already it was clear they had a lot in common.

Of course, Jessica was nice, too. She'd really gone out of her way to make him feel at home in Sweet Valley. He was glad he'd met somebody as nice as her.

But he was even more glad that her cousin had come to visit. *Robin.* Juan said the name again to himself, as their teacher entered the room and Jessica and Robin quickly took their seats behind him. Now, if only he could make Robin notice him the same way he'd noticed her. He had no idea how Americans went about this kind of thing.

I'll ask Aaron, he decided. *Aaron will know what to do.* He had heard about a dance the school was having that weekend, and the last thing he wanted was for Robin to go with someone else!

*　　*　　*

Tuesday afternoon, Robin was walking down the hall to the temporary locker Mr. Clark, the principal, had assigned to her. It felt pretty weird, going to another school in the middle of the year for two weeks. Robin wondered what she was missing at home. Probably not much, she decided. So far she was having such a good time in Sweet Valley, she was considering asking her parents to let her stay an extra two weeks.

As she neared her locker, she noticed that something had been taped to the door. She walked up and pulled off a box of candy. She stared at it for a minute, wondering who would have done such a nice thing. It had to be Elizabeth or Jessica, or one of their friends, like Mandy. Then it dawned on her. It wasn't just any box of candy—it was a box of Jujubes!

Yesterday at the Bowl-o-rama, Todd had offered to get her some, and she'd told him how much she liked them. *He remembered!* Robin thought excitedly. Not only that, but a boy just didn't leave candy for a girl he barely knew unless . . . *Unless he likes me!*

Robin quickly stuffed the Jujubes box into her backpack, then exchanged books in her locker. She started walking down the hall to her social studies class. She and Todd . . . she pictured the two of them dancing together under sparkling, shiny lights, Todd's arms wrapped around her waist. They'd have the best time together. And they could spend every waking minute together during the next eleven days . . . until he brought her to the bus station. They'd hug good-bye, and she'd climb onto the bus, tears streaming down her face, too heartbroken to even wave at him through the window. . . .

But she'd call him when she got back to San Diego, he'd write her letters, and maybe he'd come to visit, or else she'd convince her parents to let her go to Sweet Valley once a month—

"Hello. Earth to Robin. Paging Robin Wakefield," Jessica said, waving her hand in front of Robin's face. Robin had arrived at the social studies classroom in a complete trance—she hadn't noticed Jessica standing outside the room.

"Oh, hi, Jessica," Robin said. "Sorry—guess I spaced out for a minute."

"Well, you'd better wake up, fast," Jessica said. "The Hairnet will probably call on you, even if you are from out of town. I think she's trying for the Most Annoying Teacher in Sweet Valley award."

Robin laughed. Mrs. Arnette was nicknamed "the Hairnet" because she wore a hairnet around her bun. She'd made a big deal about Robin's keeping up with her class while she was in town. "I don't tolerate slackers," she'd announced in a very serious tone.

"OK, space cadet. We'd better sit down before we get into trouble," Jessica said, pulling Robin into the room by the sleeve of her sweater as the final bell rang.

Robin glanced over at where Todd had been sitting the day before. He looked up and smiled at her. Robin felt as if she were going to faint. She couldn't believe how perfectly everything was working out! She was about to go over to talk to Todd, when Mrs. Arnette rapped a ruler against the desk.

"People, take your seats now," she said sternly. "Anyone not in their seat in the next five seconds can spend the afternoon in detention."

Robin and Jessica hustled to their desks. As she slid into her seat, Robin unzipped the outside pocket of her backpack to get a notebook and pen. As she pulled them out, a piece of paper fluttered to the floor. She picked it up and read it.

"Robin," it said in very neat handwriting. "I am so glad you came to Sweet Valley. I look forward to getting to know you better." The note wasn't signed, but Robin didn't have any doubt who had written it. She was a little surprised that Todd would use such formal language, especially since they already kind of knew each other. But if he wanted to write her a note, she didn't care how he phrased it. He could use big words, fingerpaint, even write it in another language. It all meant the same thing. Todd liked her!

Robin glanced over at him, trying to get his attention, to let him know she'd gotten his note and the candy, too. But Todd was staring straight ahead, listening carefully to Mrs. Arnette's lecture.

Good-looking, thoughtful, considerate, a great athlete, and a good student, too . . . my friends in San Diego aren't going to believe this! Robin could hardly believe it herself.

*   *   *

"I don't see anything I really like, do you?" Lila asked Jessica later that afternoon at the mall. Robin and Elizabeth had gone for a bike ride with a bunch of Elizabeth's friends.

"Talk about a dry spell," Jessica said, frowning. She and Lila had already been to all their favorite stores, and Jessica hadn't seen one outfit she was in love with or felt she absolutely had to have. "There hasn't been anything good here all month."

"I'll have to talk Daddy into taking us all to L.A. for a shopping trip next weekend," Lila said.

"Definitely! That would be fantastic," Jessica said. Having a best friend who was disgustingly rich came in very handy sometimes. "The only problem is, that'll be *after* the dance," she added as they walked by Casey's. "Hey, do you want to grab a cone?"

Lila nodded. "Shopping always makes me hungry."

She and Jessica walked into Casey's and ordered frozen yogurt cones, then took a seat at a table by the window.

Jessica took a lick of her blueberry cheesecake yogurt. "So what do you think you'll wear Friday night?"

Lila shook her head. "I don't have a clue."

"I have to think of something really pretty," Jessica said wistfully, taking another lick. "Juan seems like the kind of guy who likes girls to look soft and romantic, since I'm sure he's totally romantic himself. Of course, he's so incredibly nice, he'd probably think whatever I wore was just fine. Oh, my gosh, he's going to look so amazing in a suit. . . ."

"There's only one problem with this picture," Lila cut in. "Have you actually asked him to go with you yet?"

"Well . . . no," Jessica said.

"Well, what exactly are you waiting for?" Lila demanded. "An earthquake? A sign? Courage?"

"I'm going to ask him," Jessica said defensively. "Some things just can't be rushed."

"Well, the dance is only four days away. You'd better start rushing," Lila recommended. "What makes you think he's going to wait for you?"

"Gee, thanks for the support!" Jessica snapped. "Are you saying there's someone he'd rather go with?" Robin's face flashed through her mind, but she pushed it away. She hadn't seen them talking together once that day, except that morning in homeroom when she was there. If he really liked Robin, Juan would probably let her know that. So he obviously didn't. And who else was there who could compete with Jessica?

"No, of course not," Lila said. "I just don't want to see you disappointed, that's all. How come you're putting it off?"

Jessica let out her breath. "I don't know. I guess . . . I'm just not used to asking guys out. I mean, what if I ask him and he says no?"

"Listen, Jessica, you're a Unicorn," Lila said

with emphasis. "That means if you want something you have to go for it. You can't just sit around
and wait for things to happen to you."

"Yeah, you're right," Jessica said. "I just want to
wait for the right time."

"And that would be . . . when? The year two
thousand fifty?" Lila asked.

"No," Jessica said with a laugh. "I'll ask him
soon. Very soon."

"How about tomorrow?" Lila suggested, taking a bite of her waffle cone. "Or you could call
him tonight."

"I don't think Aaron would appreciate that very
much," Jessica said.

Lila arched an eyebrow. "Does he know you like
Juan?"

Jessica nodded. "I think he's kind of getting the
message. I don't know what the big deal is. I mean,
it's not like Aaron and I are a *couple* or anything."

"You're heartless," Lila said, shaking her head.

Jessica smiled and took another lick of her ice
cream cone. She wasn't heartless at all—she just
didn't plan on being tied to one boy for the rest of her
life, the way Elizabeth was. Playing the field might be
a little harder, but it was so much more exciting!

I will ask Juan tomorrow, she told herself. *Lila's
right—I can't put it off any longer.* Then, if Juan said yes,
she could get down to the serious business of planning their date. The first date of many to come . . .

Six

◇

"You're not going to believe this when I tell you," Robin said Tuesday evening, when she and the twins had some privacy in the living room before dinner. Steven wasn't home yet—he'd said he was going to stay away as long as he could—and Mr. and Mrs. Wakefield were preparing dinner in the kitchen.

"What?" Elizabeth asked.

"I have some big news," Robin said. "Really big."

"Really? I was with you all afternoon," Elizabeth said. "Have you been holding out on me?"

"No," Robin said, smiling. "I just wanted to wait until the three of us were together."

"Well, here we are," Jessica said. "I know—this has to be about your mystery guy, doesn't it? I can tell by the look on your face." *Maybe Robin got a*

date with somebody today, she thought hopefully.
Somebody who's not Juan Valencia! If that was true,
she could go ahead and ask Juan to the dance tomorrow, as she had planned.

"He's the nicest, sweetest guy on the planet,"
Robin said, laying her head on the armrest of the
couch.

"And his name is . . ." Elizabeth prompted.

"First, he left me a box of candy, taped onto my
locker," Robin continued dreamily, as though she
hadn't heard Elizabeth. "Then he must have tucked
a note into my backpack, although I can't imagine
how. Anyway, it's a really sweet note, about how
he wants to get to know me and—"

"Wow! That's so exciting," Elizabeth said. "So
then what? Did you write him back? Did you ask
him to the dance?"

Jessica moved up to the edge of her chair. "Yeah,
did you?"

Robin shook her head, and her short blond
hair swirled around her face. "Not yet, but I'm
dying to."

"Well, what are you waiting for?" Elizabeth said.
"It's obvious he'd say yes."

Jessica was starting to have a very bad feeling
about all of this. A boy who left presents and sent
notes? That sure didn't sound like anyone she
knew. Whoever liked Robin really had a crush on
her. She thought about the way Juan had stared at
Robin all Monday afternoon at the Bowl-o-rama.

"What did the note sound like?" she asked. "What did it say, I mean?"

"Not much," Robin said. "Just that he was glad I'd come to town, and how he wanted to get to know me."

"Hmm." Jessica briefly mulled that information over. That didn't sound like Juan—but then again, she'd never gotten a note from him. "And you still don't want to tell us who this mystery guy is?"

Robin shook her head. "Not until I'm sure things are going to work out. I just feel . . . kind of superstitious. Like everything's turning out the way you predicted, Jessica, and if I do anything I might mess it up."

Why did I ever predict anything? Jessica thought, irritated with herself. *If I hadn't made Robin think she was going to fall in love here, she probably wouldn't have!*

"Well, don't leave us completely in the dark," Elizabeth urged. "Come on, give us another hint. We already know he has brown eyes and he's a good athlete."

And we already know that's not a good sign, Jessica thought.

Robin hugged her knees to her chest. "Well, let me see . . . He has dark hair, he's tall . . ."

"That could be a hundred boys at school," Elizabeth protested.

"You didn't let me finish! *And*, his first name is only one syllable," Robin said dramatically.

Elizabeth threw up her hands. "That doesn't

help! It could be Bob, Tom, Tim, Jack, John—"

Juan, Jessica thought dismally. *It could be Juan. What am I saying, could be? It* had *to be.*

"As soon as I ask him to the dance and he accepts, I'll tell you his name," Robin promised. "But not until then."

Jessica sank back in her chair, feeling completely demoralized. Brown eyes, dark hair, tall, a good athlete, a one-syllable first name. And somebody who just happened to have looked pretty excited to see Robin that morning in homeroom.

But there was one thing she really didn't understand. How could her cousin go after a boy when she knew that Jessica liked him? That didn't seem like Robin at all.

All she knew was, she'd have to get up pretty early to make it to school before Robin. She had to find Juan and ask him to the dance before Robin had a chance to.

Steven was halfway through his biology homework when there was a knock at his door. "Who is it?" he called out.

"It's me," Jessica replied.

"Go away," Steven said.

"Come on, Steven—I need your help," Jessica pleaded.

Steven walked over to the door and reluctantly opened it. "What's the matter? Can't you accessorize all by yourself?"

"Come on, this is serious." Jessica marched into his room, swept a bunch of clothes off his bed, and sat down. "I have a major problem to deal with."

Steven went back to his desk. "And I'm supposed to help you? After you've been even more annoying than usual the past four days?"

"You're counting the days?" Jessica asked, looking surprised. "Steven, why don't you get a life?"

"I thought you wanted my help?" Steven asked.

"Sorry," Jessica apologized. "I'm in a bad mood. I didn't mean to take it out on you."

Steven shrugged. "What's the big problem, anyway? I have to get back to work—we're having a huge test on Friday."

"OK, well, it's like this." Jessica took a deep breath. "There's this boy at school named Juan, and he's totally cute."

Steven drummed his fingers against his desk. He had a feeling he didn't want to know any more than that. "Uh-huh."

"And I really like him," Jessica went on. "And when Robin first got here and we all talked about asking boys to this dance on Friday, I *told* Robin and Elizabeth that I wanted to ask Juan. They both know that I like him. Only now, all of a sudden, Robin's decided that she likes Juan, and she's going to ask him to the dance. I don't know what to do!"

Steven stared at her. "And that's your big problem? That's what you interrupted me for?"

"Steven, come on—what should I do?" Jessica

asked. "It's not fair that she's asking Juan out when I'm the one who wanted to first. I mean, she didn't even know who he *was* until I introduced them yesterday!"

Steven was about to tell Jessica that this was the most ridiculous thing he'd ever heard. He didn't care who went to the dance with whom or if they went at all—except it meant they'd be out of the house for once. But Jessica looked genuinely upset, and she had the intelligence, for once, to rely on him for advice. He did know a thing or two about dating. He'd had his share of heartbreak. "There's only one thing you can do," he told Jessica.

Jessica looked eagerly at him. "What?"

"Tell Robin you're the one who liked him first," Steven said. "Simple as that."

"And do you think that'll work?" Jessica sounded skeptical.

"Sure," Steven said. "Not that it's ever worked for me, but you never know. Robin might back off."

"And if she doesn't, then what?" Jessica said.

"Then . . . you go with somebody else," Steven said. "It's not like that would be the end of the world, you know."

Jessica stood up, shaking her head. "You don't understand! It would be!"

"Jessica, get a grip," Steven said. "It's only one dance out of, like, two thousand."

"It's not just one dance. It's about me and Robin and our friendship, and I really like this guy and—"

"Never mind, then!" Steven cried. "I'm sure my advice is totally worthless, I don't know anything that could help you, so stop wasting my time and get out of here!"

"Stop wasting *your* time? You're the one with the lousy advice!" Jessica replied.

"So why did you come here in the first place, if I always give such lousy advice?" Steven retorted.

"I don't know. I must be crazy to think *you* could help me!" Jessica said angrily, opening the door.

"Good—we finally agree on something! You are crazy!" Steven cried.

"Probably because I'm related to you!" Jessica shot back, just before slamming the door.

Steven sighed, frustrated, and turned back to the homework on his desk. What next? Was Robin going to come in and ask what she should do, since she liked the same boy? And then what—would Elizabeth come to his room and start whining about her love life, too?

Steven went over to his door and flipped the lock on the back of the doorknob. He wasn't taking any chances.

Jessica pulled her comforter up tightly around her neck and peered across the room at Robin, who was sleeping on a cot next to her bed. Only, Robin wasn't sleeping, either—her eyes were wide open. Jessica fluffed up her pillow, punching it a few times, then settled back down. As hard as she tried, though, she couldn't fall asleep. She had to know whether the mystery guy Robin kept talking about was Juan. If she didn't ask her, she would lie awake all night and look terrible in the morning. Juan would never say yes to her in that case.

She didn't want to come right out and accuse Robin of trying to steal her boyfriend, but at the moment, she didn't see any other choice but to demand an explanation—and some answers.

"Robin? Are you asleep?" Jessica asked.

"No," Robin said. "I'm too wound up to sleep. I keep thinking about—"

"I know, I know, about your wonderful mystery boyfriend." Jessica sat up in bed and whipped off the covers. "Listen, Robin, I have to know who this person is, and the suspense is killing me, because I have a horrible feeling we want to ask the same boy. Which I personally can't believe, since I told you when you got here that I was asking Juan, so if you are, too, then we have a serious problem on our hands, and you might want to sleep in Elizabeth's room because—"

Robin sat up in bed, her hair falling in her face. "But Jessica, I—"

"Don't even try to tell me you didn't know I liked Juan, because I told you the second you stepped off that bus that I was going to ask him, and I know you heard me, because we talked about it more than once, so don't try to tell me you don't know—"

"I did know!" Robin protested. "And I'd never—"

"Aha! So you admit it! You did know! You do know! And you went ahead and tried to sneak in between me and Juan, which isn't exactly how I go around treating my friends, and I always thought you were my friend, plus my cousin, which makes it *twice* as bad—"

"Jessica!" Robin screamed. "Shut up!"

Jessica stopped talking and looked over at Robin. "What did you just say to me?"

"Stop talking long enough so I can tell you that I'm *not* planning on asking Juan to the dance Friday!" Robin declared.

"You're not?" Jessica jumped up out of bed. "You're not! She's not asking Juan!" She started doing a little dance around the bedroom.

"I'd never try to horn in on somebody you liked," Robin said. "How could you even think that about me?"

"I didn't want to," Jessica replied. "But all the clues you gave—the brown eyes, being tall, having a one-syllable name. Who else could it be?"

"I guess I can see how you thought it was Juan," Robin said. "He's really cute, but Jessica, I'd never go after your boyfriend."

"He's not my boyfriend," Jessica said. "Yet. But wait a second—if it's not Juan, then who could it possibly be?"

"Well . . ."

"You have to tell me, this instant!" Jessica demanded. "Because it sure doesn't sound like any-body else at school I know!"

"But you do know him," Robin said slowly. "It's Todd."

"T-Todd?" Jessica sputtered. "Todd Wilkins?" He might have brown eyes, but they were nothing like Juan's. How could anyone besides Elizabeth think he was so wonderful? Spending time with Todd was about as much fun as doing homework.

"You sound shocked," Robin observed.

"Well, I . . ." Jessica hesitated. She didn't know what to say. Robin was right about Jessica's reaction, though—she *was* completely shocked.

"What's the matter? Does he already have a girl-friend or something? Is that why you're acting so weird?" Robin asked.

"Well, actually—" Jessica began, then stopped abruptly. *Wait a minute,* she thought, as she remembered again how Juan acted around Robin. *So she doesn't like* him, *but there's still a chance that he likes* her. But if she went to the dance with Todd, Juan would see she was off-limits. He'd forget all about her—and start focusing on Jessica, the way he was supposed to.

Besides, Todd and Robin's date would break up Todd and Elizabeth, which could only be good for Elizabeth in the long run. Elizabeth could do much better, and have a lot more fun, if only she'd start dating other boys. Only, Elizabeth couldn't see that for herself. She obviously needed help.

So if Robin *did* manage to go out with Todd, Elizabeth would be minus one very boring boyfriend. Sure, it might hurt her twin a little bit to break up with Todd, but Jessica was looking at the big picture—something Elizabeth could never see.

Of course, that was just the bonus. The best part was that Jessica would get to go to the dance with Juan, the way she'd planned all along.

"Jessica!" Robin shrieked impatiently. "You *have* to tell me! Does Todd have a girlfriend or not?"

"Actually? Todd's not dating anyone right now," Jessica told Robin, putting her arm around her cousin's shoulders. "And you know what? I think you two will make a great couple."

"Really?" Robin asked.

"Really," Jessica said.

"But don't tell Elizabeth yet, OK? I'm still worried about jinxing the whole thing," Robin said. "You won't tell her, will you?"

"No," Jessica said, smiling. "I definitely won't tell Elizabeth. You can count on me."

Seven

"Hi, Elizabeth." Todd leaned against the locker next to Elizabeth's. "Where have you been?" It was Wednesday morning just before lunch, and Elizabeth was on her way to the *Sixers* office.

"Working on the newspaper—what else?" Elizabeth replied, smiling at him. "I have to head up there now and check the layout on the computer." She adjusted the ribbon tied around her ponytail.

"That's what you've been saying all week. Every time I want to talk to you, you're on your way to the *Sixers* office," Todd said, pushing up the sleeves of his rugby shirt. "I'm starting to think you're trying to ignore me."

Elizabeth felt terrible—Todd looked pretty upset. Had she really been ignoring him? "You don't really think that—"

"No, I was just joking," Todd said, breaking into a smile. "But it would be fun to do something together this week—you know, *before* Friday night."

Elizabeth gave him a teasing smile. "Friday? What happens Friday night?" she asked, pretending not to know about the dance.

"I think you're supposed to invite me to something." Todd tapped his chin. "Hmm, I can't remember exactly *what*, though. But I think it's happening somewhere near here . . . the gym, maybe?"

"Is it a pickup basketball game?" Elizabeth asked, fiddling with the lock on her locker.

"No, I don't think it has anything to do with basketball," Todd said thoughtfully.

"Oh. Well, when you remember what it is, you'll tell me, right?" Elizabeth teased.

"Oh, sure. If you don't remember first," Todd said.

"Of course." Elizabeth grinned at him. She really hadn't seen much of Todd all week—she hadn't realized it before, but she missed him. "Hey, you know what? If I work on the paper now, and spend my lunch hour working on it, too, I think I could probably take this afternoon off," Elizabeth said. "We could go to Casey's together and split a sundae. Maybe the hot fudge will jar my memory, and I'll remember what I'm supposed to ask you."

Todd smiled. "That sounds like a great idea."

"Meet me by the front steps?" Elizabeth asked.

"OK. Sounds good," Todd replied, nodding. He

started to walk away, then turned back. "Maybe the sundae will even be my treat."

Elizabeth blushed. "That would be really nice. And, um . . . in that case, do you think I could have my own?"

"Go finish that *Sixers* edition without breaking the computer, and we'll see," Todd told her.

Elizabeth laughed. "OK, it's a deal."

After her last class, Robin headed toward her locker to grab the books she needed to do her homework that night. She'd never been so glad that the school day was over. First Mrs. Arnette had made her come up to the front of the class and talk about the history of San Diego—as if she knew enough to talk for more than five minutes—then she'd had a quiz in science that she had to have bombed. She couldn't wait to just go home, hang out, and—

"What? Another note?" Robin peeled off a piece of notebook paper that had been taped to her locker.

"Dear Robin," she read out loud. "We didn't get a chance to talk today. I missed seeing you. But I am still thinking about you. Signed, your secret admirer."

"Secret admirer?" Robin scoffed. "Hardly!" Did Todd think she really didn't know how he felt about her?

"Are you talking to yourself?"

Robin looked up to see Jessica standing in front

of her. She hadn't even noticed her cousin come up. "Sorry—I was just reading this note from my so-called secret admirer."

"Let me see!" Jessica said eagerly. She took the paper from Robin and quickly read it. When she was done, she handed it back to Robin, frowning.

"What's wrong? Isn't it sweet?" Robin asked.

"Oh, yeah," Jessica muttered. "It's sweet, all right." She cleared her throat. "No, it's great, really. So does this mean you haven't asked Todd to the dance yet?"

"Not yet." Robin felt her stomach flip-flop. Just the thought of asking Todd made her nervous—she didn't know how she could actually go through with it. But then she pictured the two of them dancing together. She had to ask him. Today.

"You should definitely ask him soon," Jessica said firmly. "The sooner the better, actually. Why don't you find him now?"

"Do you really think he'd say yes?" Robin asked.

"He's sending you all the right signals, isn't he? He obviously wants you to ask him. You have to go for it!"

"Seize the day?" Robin said tentatively.

"Exactly," Jessica agreed. "Look, I have to go to pep squad practice. You find Todd, and I'll meet you at home later this afternoon, OK?"

Robin nodded. "OK. I'll see you later. Wish me luck."

"Oh, I do," Jessica said. "More than you could

ever imagine. Bye!" She ran off down the hall, and Robin started looking around for Todd. She saw Juan standing by his locker, and Mandy, and almost everyone else who went to Sweet Valley Middle School—just not Todd. *Where is he? If I don't find him soon, I'm going to lose my nerve!*

She was wandering toward the front door when Aaron ran past her, wearing his soccer practice clothes. "Hey, Aaron!" she called after him. "Have you seen Todd?"

Aaron turned around, jogging backward. "No, but I think he was heading to Casey's after school. You know, at the mall? I have to run or I'll miss practice. See you later!"

Robin grinned. "Thanks!" She was pretty sure she remembered how to get there—Jessica and Elizabeth had brought her there on Sunday. Casey's would be the perfect setting to ask Todd to the dance. They could sit at a booth and talk in private. Maybe they could even share a sundae.

Only a few more minutes and Todd will stop being my secret admirer—and start being my boyfriend!

"That is the hugest sundae I've ever seen in my life!" Elizabeth said, sliding into the booth next to Todd. She handed him one of the long spoons she'd picked up at the counter.

"Don't worry, we'll finish it," Todd said, digging into the Triple Brownie Tower of Fudge—one of Casey's famous specials. "Here, you should have the first bite." He held the gooey spoon out to Elizabeth.

"Mm," she said. "Thanks."

"This hot fudge is amazing," Todd said, digging up a spoonful for himself.

"I think we're going to go into sugar shock in a minute," Elizabeth said with a laugh after having another bite. "So how has your week been?"

Todd shrugged. "OK, I guess. Same old stuff. How about you?"

"Well, besides working on the special edition, I've been spending a lot of time with Robin," Elizabeth explained. "You know how it is when someone's visiting—especially someone you really like to hang out with, like Robin."

"Yeah, I know," Todd said. "She's really nice. I just wish you and I could have . . . I don't know. Done more together. You know?"

Elizabeth nodded. "You don't think I was avoiding you or anything, do you?"

Todd shook his head and held out another bite of ice cream toward Elizabeth. "It just seemed like . . . maybe you were putting off asking me something?"

"Asking you something?" Elizabeth repeated, her eyes wide with innocence. "What do you mean?"

"Oh, nothing important," Todd said, looking around Casey's and leaning back casually in his seat. "I'm just wondering if you're going to have fun at that dance, all by yourself. I'm sure you will. I bet you'll have a great time, talking to everyone."

Todd cleared his throat. "Of course, if you decide you'd rather not dance alone, I happen to know this guy who's a really good dancer—well, at least he's not a really *bad* dancer—and he could, you know, probably make the evening a lot more fun. He might still be available—I'm not sure."

"Really. Is that so?" Elizabeth picked up a bite of brownie in her spoon and held it out to Todd. "So enough kidding around," she said, gazing into Todd's eyes. "I *have* been putting this off forever, but not because I didn't know I wanted to ask— Oh, hey, there's Robin." She pointed to the doorway.

"What's she doing here?" Elizabeth wondered. "I thought she was spending the afternoon with Jessica."

Robin had practically run the whole way to the Valley Mall. Once she made up her mind to ask Todd to the dance, she could hardly wait. *Jessica's right,* she thought. *I just have to go for it.*

She glanced quickly at the mall directory just inside the door, then hurried down the wing that led to Casey's, almost knocking over an older man who stepped out of a store and stood right in front of her.

"I'm sorry—excuse me," she said quickly.

"Watch where you're going," he grumbled at her.

Normally Robin would have stopped to apologize further, but she just didn't have the patience today. She was on a mission. Finally! There it was!

She skidded to a stop in the doorway of Casey's.

She looked around, checking each booth and table for Todd. At first she didn't see him anywhere. Then she caught a glance of his dark-brown hair—she couldn't quite be sure it was him, so she took a couple of steps into the restaurant.

That looked like Todd, but it was hard to see, because someone was blocking his face. A girl. A girl who was sitting in his booth—on the same side of the booth he was! Robin stared as the girl lifted a spoonful of ice cream to Todd's lips. Who was that? Why was Todd with another girl? She felt as though her head were spinning.

The girl looked up and smiled at her. Robin felt her heart drop into her Doc Martens. *Elizabeth?*

What was Elizabeth doing with *her* secret admirer, *her* boyfriend? How could she do that to Robin?

Elizabeth's face lit up when she saw Robin, and Todd waved. Robin gave them both a long, horrified stare. *How dare they sit there together and act friendly to me—after what they've done!*

She turned around and ran out of Casey's as fast as she could. Was Todd just playing with her feelings? That couldn't be true. He was too nice to do that. And anyway, Elizabeth was the one who was feeding *him* ice cream and flirting with him.

Robin yanked open the side door of the mall and started sprinting home. How could her very own cousin set out to steal the love of *her* life? She didn't want to see Elizabeth again as long as she lived!

Eight

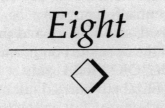

"She looked really upset," Elizabeth commented to Todd when Robin ran out of Casey's. "Why did she take off like that?"

"I don't know," Todd said. "You'd think she would at least come over and say hello to us."

"Something must be wrong." Elizabeth furrowed her brow. "Maybe she was looking for me, but she didn't want to talk to me with you around." She thought about Robin's secret admirer. Maybe she had asked him to the dance—and he had turned her down! Robin had her hopes up so high, she would be crushed if that happened. And she wouldn't want to talk about it front of another boy. That had to be it. "I think I know what's bothering her," she told Todd. "Look, I hate to cut our date short, but I want to go home and make sure she's all right. Who knows where Jessica is, and my parents won't be home until five and—"

"That's OK," Todd said. "You don't have to explain. I understand."

"You're the greatest. But if you finish this sundae all by yourself, you may be the sickest," Elizabeth warned, standing up and picking up her backpack from the opposite booth bench.

"See you later, OK?" Todd said.

"OK. Bye!" Elizabeth hurried out of Casey's and started running home as fast as she could. She was moving so quickly, she couldn't believe she didn't see Robin anywhere along the way. Robin had to have really rushed to outrun her. *I hope she's at home,* she thought. *I hope she didn't go back to school to find Jessica or something.*

About fifteen minutes later, Elizabeth ran up her driveway. She quickly unlocked the front door and went into the house. "Robin?" she called. "Are you here?" She searched the living room and dining room, then walked into the kitchen.

Robin was leaning against the refrigerator, drinking a glass of water. Her cheeks were streaked with tears.

"I'm so glad I found you!" Elizabeth said, rushing to her side. "Are you all right? What happened?"

"What *happened*? How can you even have the nerve to ask me that?" Robin replied. She sounded furious.

"What do you mean?" Elizabeth asked, confused.

"What I mean is, Elizabeth, how could you do something like that to me?" Robin demanded.

"Something like . . . what?"

"Come on, stop pretending you don't know. You deliberately stole my boyfriend, and now you're going to act all innocent about it?" Robin shook her head and dumped the rest of the water in her glass into the sink.

Elizabeth was completely dumbfounded. What was Robin talking about? Stealing her boyfriend? Since when was Todd Robin's boyfriend?

Wait a minute . . . Elizabeth thought about all the clues Robin had given her and Jessica about her mystery boy: brown eyes, dark hair, a great athlete . . . his first name was only one syllable. "Todd?" she whispered.

"Yes, *Todd*," Robin said angrily.

"But I didn't know— I thought you liked somebody else—but not—never—"

Robin laughed. "Nice try, Elizabeth. You knew Todd was the only guy I ever liked! So how could you steal him from me?"

"I didn't steal him from you," Elizabeth protested. Didn't Robin know that she and Todd were dating? She must have misinterpreted Todd's being nice to her as a sign that he liked her. "Listen, Robin. Todd and I— You must not have understood."

Robin put her glass into the sink. "Oh, I *understand*, all right. Don't bother explaining or making up some lame excuse for what I saw you doing at Casey's," she said. "Flirting with Todd to try to get him to like you more than he likes me. Well, it's not going to work, so you might as well give up."

"Give—give up?" Elizabeth stammered.

"Todd's mine," Robin said. "You're not going to steal him from me. I'm not going to give him up without a fight, and as far as I'm concerned, from now on it's war between us!" She walked straight past Elizabeth, head held high even though a tear was rolling down her cheek.

Elizabeth just stood in the kitchen, completely stunned, as she heard Robin go upstairs and slam Jessica's bedroom door closed behind her. *A war— between me and Robin . . . for Todd?*

What's going on?

"Jessica. Come in here for a second." Robin beckoned to Jessica from the downstairs den.

"Why?" Jessica asked. "What's up?"

"I've been dying for you to get home. You are not going to believe what happened this afternoon. I mean, it's absolutely incredible, and it's all Elizabeth's rotten fault." Robin forced herself to whisper even though she still felt like shouting. Everyone was in the dining room about to start eating dinner, and she didn't want them all to know what a creep of a daughter and sister they had.

"What are you talking about?" Jessica drew Robin farther into the den.

"Elizabeth. And Todd. Together," Robin said meaningfully.

"Huh?" Jessica asked, looking surprised.

"I went to Casey's to find Todd, to ask him to the dance like you suggested," Robin explained. Just remembering what had happened made her blood boil all over again. It was so humiliating. And so aggravating! "Only, instead of finding Todd alone, I found Elizabeth with him—sitting *right* next to him, flirting with him, putting this spoonful of ice cream in his mouth—"

"Ick." Jessica made a face. "How disgusting."

"How *rude* is what you mean," Robin said. "Can you believe she'd have the nerve to try to steal Todd? I mean, she must have figured out that he was the one I liked, and then—boom! She's right after him like a shot. She was probably going to ask him to the dance, if I hadn't shown up and ruined her big moment."

"Wow," Jessica said. "That's terrible! It's appalling!"

"Have you ever known Elizabeth to do something like this?" Robin asked. "I always thought she was so kind and thoughtful. . . ."

"Well, there's a side to Elizabeth that a lot of people don't know," Jessica said in a serious tone. "Still, what she did *is* pretty harsh. What did you *say* to her? Did she try to explain?"

"She tried, but I wasn't about to listen," Robin said, folding her arms. "I told her that the way I see it, this means war. The winner gets Todd."

A small smile flickered at the corners of Jessica's mouth.

"Why are you smiling?" Robin asked.

"Oh . . . it's just that I was thinking about how great it's going to be when you win that war," Jessica said. "And to make sure you do, I think there are a few things I can do to help. I can't promise anything, but I'll do what I can."

"Will you really?" Robin threw her arms around Jessica and hugged her. "You're the best cousin, even if your sister's a jerk." She stepped back. "Are you sure you want to choose my side? I mean, Elizabeth is your twin."

"But you're my favorite cousin, and you didn't come to visit me just to have your heart stomped all over," Jessica said. "I want to be on your side. Trust me."

"Thanks, Jessica," Robin said gratefully, wiping away a tear that had welled up. "Oh, my gosh—I forgot to ask—did you ask Juan to the dance today?"

"No . . . but I'm going to ask him tomorrow. I know that for a fact!" Jessica declared confidently.

"Jessica! You're really leaving it until the last minute!" Robin scolded her.

"No, I was just waiting for the right time, that's all. And I have a very good feeling about tomorrow," Jessica replied calmly. "A very good feeling."

*   *   *

Jessica pulled back her chair at the dining table and sat down. Across the table, Elizabeth was fiddling with her silverware, not looking up. Robin sat beside Jessica.

"Where's Steven tonight?" Jessica asked.

"Having pizza with some friends," her father said. "He said something about how it would save his sanity."

"Well, don't worry, Uncle Ned," Robin said. "We won't bother Steven tonight. We won't be staying up late and we won't be making any noise at all." She gave a pointed look at Elizabeth, who met her gaze, then looked down at her plate.

Jessica unfolded her napkin and picked up the tray of tacos in front of her. She took a couple and put them on her plate, then passed the tray to Robin. She was starving. When things went well, she always got extra-hungry.

She knew that sending Robin after Todd had been a little risky—after all, there was a small chance that Todd would tell Robin the truth about him and Elizabeth and that Robin would believe him and get mad at Jessica. But she'd had a feeling that instead Robin would just fight harder for Todd, and it looked as if things had worked out just as Jessica had hoped. A little more work, and Todd would be Robin's date for the dance . . . which meant Juan would be hers. It would all happen tomorrow, with a little extra effort on her part.

"Only one taco, Elizabeth?" Mrs. Wakefield asked. "I thought these were your favorite."

Elizabeth shrugged her shoulders. "I guess I'm not that hungry."

"Must have been that sundae you had at Casey's," Robin said in a superior tone.

"Actually, I didn't get the chance to finish it," Elizabeth replied snootily.

"What are you two talking about?" Mrs. Wakefield asked.

"It's nothing, Mom," Jessica said nervously. The last thing she wanted was for her mother to find out what was going on. Her mother had this weird sixth sense—whenever Jessica did something wrong, her mother could somehow just *tell*. She'd know right away who was behind everything, and that Jessica had encouraged Robin to go after Elizabeth's boyfriend. "They're just joking, aren't you, guys?"

Elizabeth glared at Robin, then started eating. Robin tapped her fork against her plate, then took a bite of the refried beans.

Jessica felt an unexpected twinge of guilt. It was kind of sad to see Robin and Elizabeth so angry at each other. They had always been such good, close friends. Maybe the dance wasn't worth all this, after all.

Then Jessica pictured herself in Juan's arms at the dance Friday night. She was wearing a beautiful dress and he was gazing at her with his gorgeous eyes.

Yes, Jessica decided, *the dance is definitely worth it.*

Nine

"Hurry up, Jessica," Robin urged on Thursday morning. "Remember, the sooner you get to school, the sooner you can ask Juan to the dance."

Jessica dug through the clothes on her closet floor. "Just a second."

"You're already dressed—what are you looking for?" Robin sat on the bed and tapped her foot against the floor impatiently.

Jessica tried to remember what Elizabeth had worn to school that morning. She'd left early, before breakfast, and Jessica had only caught a glimpse of her going down the sidewalk. But she was pretty sure Elizabeth was wearing a red sweater and blue jeans. Jessica finally found her red cardigan and stuffed it into her backpack. "OK, I'm all set." She stood up and turned to face Robin.

They went downstairs and headed outside for the short walk to school.

"I am so exhausted," Robin said as they went down the sidewalk. "I couldn't sleep at all last night."

"Why not?" Jessica asked, glancing both ways before they crossed the street.

"Elizabeth," Robin said. "I kept thinking about how I saw her and Todd together, and how awful she was to pull a stunt like that on me. I mean, she's supposed to be my cousin."

"Well . . ." Jessica paused. It was hard for her not to feel a little guilty about what she was doing to Elizabeth—and Robin. It probably wasn't fair to either of them, or even to Todd, as boring as he was. But was it fair for Robin to waltz into town and draw all of Juan's attention away from her? No. Was it fair that she should lose the love of her life because of a poorly timed visit? "I'm sure Elizabeth will come around and apologize, as soon as she gets over it," Jessica said. "Anyway, she was probably just confused."

"Confused is right," Robin said. "She actually thought Todd liked her! When I know for a fact he likes me. I mean, who else has been sending me love notes, giving me presents . . ."

Who else but Juan? Jessica thought with a frown. She couldn't get over the fact that Juan was still sending notes to Robin. She'd seen his handwriting the day before on the note Robin showed her—she recognized it from the time she tried to help Juan with some homework. How could he like Robin when she liked someone else—and how could he not notice that he risked ruining his chances with Jessica by pursuing Robin?

Boys, Jessica thought. *They just don't get it!*

But with her help, they were all going to figure out who they were supposed to take to the dance. They just needed her . . . advice, that was all. Was it her fault she was smarter about these love and dating things than anybody else?

Pretty soon, Juan would be sending love notes to *her* instead of Robin. And it was about time.

Jessica hovered outside the library, trying to catch a glimpse of Todd. It was fourth period, and she was supposed to be in the language lab, practicing her French, but she knew this was the only time she could catch Todd alone. She'd asked Aaron about his schedule, saying she needed to return something he'd left at their house.

She hurried into the bathroom, pulled the red cardigan out of her backpack, and slipped it on over her blouse. Then she brushed her hair and pulled it back in a ponytail. Jessica had gotten a chance to check out Elizabeth's outfit in homeroom that morning, and though she knew she wouldn't look exactly the same, she was pretty close.

As if Todd would remember what Elizabeth was wearing! As far as she could tell, the two hadn't even exchanged a word in homeroom or all morning. Apparently, Elizabeth was so upset about what had happened with Robin that she didn't even want to talk to Todd.

And that's just going to help my impersonation even more, Jessica thought, smiling confidently at her reflection in the mirror. *One Elizabeth Wakefield scene, coming up.*

She went back to the library and walked straight over to the table where Todd was sitting.

"Hi, Elizabeth!" Todd whispered excitedly when Jessica sat down next to him. "What was wrong with Robin yesterday? And why didn't you talk to me in homeroom?" He frowned. "And hey, weren't you wearing something different?"

What is this—twenty questions? Jessica wondered. It figured that Todd would become observant on the day she chose to try to fool him. Jessica sighed and tried to look serious the way Elizabeth would. She knit her eyebrows. "It's all a long story," she began. "First of all, I had to change my sweater because . . . the laser printer toner thing up at the newspaper came open and I got toner all over it. I borrowed this from Amy."

"Yeah, well." Todd fidgeted with his pencil. "So how come you blew me off in homeroom?"

"Well . . . I didn't know what to do, with Robin sitting right there. I didn't want to pay too much attention to you, because I was afraid it would hurt her feelings," Jessica replied.

"Huh?" Todd looked completely befuddled. "What are you talking about, Elizabeth?"

Got him, Jessica thought triumphantly. "Robin was so upset yesterday at Casey's because she saw the two of us together and she thought . . . well, she feels incredibly left out of the whole couples and dating scene. See, she's never had a boyfriend. And she's dying to go to the dance on Friday."

"So why doesn't she ask someone?" Todd suggested.

"That's just it," Jessica said, putting on her best sympathetic, Elizabeth expression. "She did ask someone, and he turned her down."

"You're kidding—who?"

Jessica shook her head. "That's not important. What matters is that she's very, very upset. She's hardly eating. She cries a lot . . . it's enough to break your heart."

"Really?" Todd said. "Robin didn't strike me as that lovesick type—you know, like Jessica."

It took all of Jessica's strength not to punch Todd in the face. Instead she smiled politely, just as Elizabeth would. "Actually, they're more alike than you'd think. But here's the thing, Todd. I have an idea. You know, I'm probably going to be too busy dealing with the whole *Sixers* mess to go to the dance—I won't have a free minute till the issue comes out on Monday." Jessica paused, glad she'd heard Elizabeth talking about the *Sixers* with her mother the night before while they washed the dishes.

"So what are you saying?" Todd asked. "You're not going to ask me to the dance?" He looked hurt.

Jessica knew she was making Todd suffer, and she knew she should feel bad, but she was kind of enjoying watching him squirm. "I'm sorry, I just don't think I can make it," she said. "But I have a great idea—it hit me just last night." She paused again, for dramatic effect.

"What is it?" Todd prompted her.

"You and Robin could go to the dance together!" Jessica announced cheerfully.

Todd paled. "No! No way, Elizabeth. If I can't go with you, I don't want to go at all."

Wow, Jessica thought. *He really likes Elizabeth. A lot.* Again, she felt that annoying twinge of guilt. She'd never realized how devoted to her sister he was. But that wasn't *her* problem, she told herself. Besides, Todd didn't really deserve special treatment just because he liked Elizabeth—everyone loved her, even the incredibly rude clerks at the grocery store.

Jessica cleared her throat. "Come on, Todd. You saw how upset Robin was yesterday. Just promise me you'll say yes if she asks you to the dance."

"But I don't want to go with her," Todd protested. "It would all be fake, anyway."

"Not really," Jessica said. "I mean, you guys get along as friends, right? And if she has a date she won't be humiliated when she sees that jerk who for some idiotic reason turned her down yesterday."

Todd raised his eyebrows in surprise.

Oops. I guess that wasn't something Elizabeth would say. "I mean, it wasn't very nice of him to hurt Robin's feelings like that. Anyway, would you please help me out and agree to go with Robin? Only, don't tell her I asked you to, OK? It would cheer her up so much. I can't take another night of seeing her so miserable," Jessica said, putting on her best concerned Elizabeth look. "It almost broke my heart, Todd. I mean, I guess I never realized how lucky we were to have each other." She smiled at him, and noticed a puppy-dog expression on his face. *If he kisses me, I really will slug him*, she thought.

"Elizabeth, you're always trying to make other people happy," Todd said, gazing into Jessica's eyes. "You're almost *too* nice."

"Well." Jessica stood up nervously. "I'd better run back to the *Sixers* office. I'll talk to you later!" She turned to leave. She had to get back into the bathroom and change before she saw anyone she or Elizabeth knew.

"Elizabeth, wait! What about lunch?" Todd called after her.

Ms. Luster, the school librarian, stepped out from behind her desk. "Please make your social plans quietly—some other time, perhaps?" she said sternly to Todd.

Jessica slipped out of the library, glad for the distraction. That had been even easier than she thought. Now she just had to find Robin before the real Elizabeth spoke to Todd.

Ten

◇

"Robin!" Jessica rushed over to the Unicorner, where Robin had just sat down to have lunch. Robin had planned to eat with Elizabeth today, but that was before their war started. She hadn't spoken to Elizabeth all day, and she didn't plan on it, either.

"Hi, Jessica." Robin broke an apple-cinnamon muffin on her tray in half. "Want some?"

Jessica crouched by her seat. "Thanks. Did you ask Todd to the dance yet?" she whispered, accepting the muffin half.

"No," Robin said. "I thought I could try to ask him in social studies this afternoon."

Jessica shook her head. "Don't wait that long! Look, he's right over there, and his friends are all still in line. Now would be the perfect time."

"I don't know—do you think so? It's kind of

public in here. If he says no . . ." Robin bit her lip.

"He's not going to!" Jessica said. She glanced at the cafeteria entrance. "And if I were you, I'd get over there before Elizabeth does. You don't want *her* to go to the dance with him, do you?"

"Is she coming?" Robin asked, looking over her shoulder.

"Yes, and she's heading over to Todd's table right now. Hurry!" Jessica urged.

Robin pushed back her chair. She wasn't about to let Elizabeth get away with asking her boyfriend to the dance. She'd said it was a war, and she meant it! Fortunately, Elizabeth had gotten stuck trying to cut through a long line of students. Robin marched over to Todd's table. "Hi, Todd," she said cheerfully. "Is it OK if I sit down for a second?"

Todd looked up at her and smiled. "Sure, Robin. Go ahead."

Robin settled into the chair opposite his. "Sorry I ran out of Casey's yesterday. I had—something on my mind."

"Oh, that's OK," Todd said kindly. "No problem."

"Anyway," Robin continued, her heart thumping hard. "I was looking for you because I wanted to ask you a question."

"Oh. OK," Todd said. "What is it?"

Robin took a deep breath. She was clenching the seat of the chair with both hands. *Here goes everything.* "I'd like to ask you to come to the dance with me this Friday. Will you please be my date?"

Todd smiled. "Sure. I'd love to go with you."

"Really?" Robin almost shrieked. "I mean, uh, really? That's great. Wow, thanks."

"You don't have to thank me," Todd said with a shrug. "I'm sure we'll have fun."

"You're right—we will," Robin said. "Todd, this is great!" She spotted Elizabeth walking toward them and raised her voice to say, "I can't tell you how much your going to the dance with me means to me!"

"I think I know," Todd said, looking up briefly at Elizabeth and scooting his chair forward so somebody could walk behind him.

"You do?" Robin was confused.

Todd cleared his throat. "I mean, it's . . . it means a lot to me, too. I'm really looking forward to it."

"Me, too," Robin said. *You have no idea how much!* She was about to thank Todd for all the nice notes and gifts he'd left for her, but a couple of his friends, Ken Matthews and Tom McKay, came over to the table, and she didn't want to embarrass him. So she thanked Todd again, then ran back to the Unicorner to tell Jessica the good news.

"What did he say?" Jessica asked eagerly.

"He said he'd *love* to go with me." Robin held up her hand, and Jessica slapped her a high five. "My date's all set now—what about yours?"

"Any minute now," Jessica said.

"You know, I have to say I'm pretty surprised Juan doesn't have a date yet," Robin remarked, sitting down next to her. "I mean, is everyone around here blind?"

"Must be," Jessica said with a shrug. "But don't worry, Robin. You've totally inspired me. I'm going to ask Juan, the next chance I get."

"Elizabeth! Elizabeth!"

Elizabeth glanced over her shoulder and kept walking. She was furious! How dare Todd even mention her name—much less run after her—after what he'd done?

She'd always thought Todd was different from other guys. That he would always be loyal to her. That she could trust him not to dump her just because someone else liked him, or because another girl was prettier or more popular than she was. Now what? The first time another girl asked him out, he said yes, right off! Without even telling her about it or talking it over with her. He obviously didn't care for Elizabeth as much as he said he did. He wasn't even brave enough to tell her in person—she had to find out by overhearing him and Robin in the middle of the school cafeteria.

Todd jogged to a stop beside her. "Elizabeth, why didn't you stop? I've been running after you, calling your name—"

"Well, you can keep *on* running," Elizabeth said angrily. "In fact, you can run right past me and never talk to me again!" She turned the corner and started up the stairs to the second floor.

"But—Elizabeth—me and Robin—" Todd protested.

"That's right! You and Robin!" Elizabeth exclaimed, fuming. "I hope you have a nice time at the dance together! Just don't tell me about it, OK?" She felt as if she were going to burst out crying, right on the stairway, surrounded by kids.

"But I didn't—"

"I know I asked you to be nice to her, but that doesn't mean you have to go overboard and—"

"I was only nice to her because you asked me to," Todd said, sounding completely befuddled.

"Well, you sure redefined the word *nice*," Elizabeth shot back. She turned toward him briefly. "Have a great time together."

"Elizabeth, I don't understand," Todd said desperately.

"Maybe that's part of the problem," Elizabeth said icily. "Now just leave *me* alone!" She turned and ran into the *Sixers* office, slamming the door behind her. She leaned back against the door and tried to catch her breath.

How could Todd turn his back on her like that? Did he think Robin was prettier than she was? Or had he gotten tired of waiting for her to ask him? Couldn't he see she was just teasing him a little, holding out like that?

"Agh!" she cried, throwing her notebook on the floor. She didn't know the answers, and right now, she didn't care. All she did know was that Todd was a major jerk.

After lunch, Robin practically floated down the hall to her locker. She and Todd were really going to the dance together. It was a dream come true. Nothing could go wrong now. No matter how much Elizabeth liked Todd, she was just going to have to accept the fact that he and Robin were an item. Elizabeth would get over her crush eventually. Robin hoped so, anyway. As angry as she had been at Elizabeth, Robin really didn't want her cousin to be unhappy. In fact, she wished everyone could be as happy as she felt right at that moment!

She could hardly wait for the dance. She'd wear the new cranberry-colored dress she'd brought, the one she'd gotten at one of the most expensive stores back home. Her mother and the salesclerk had said it made her look older and more sophisticated, and she even had shoes and jewelry to complement it perfectly. Todd was going to be swept away when he came to pick her up and saw how beautiful she looked.

Robin stopped walking, realizing she had just gone past her locker without even seeing it.

As she headed back toward her locker, she felt a jolt of surprise. Was that *another* thing taped to her locker? Why hadn't Todd just given it to her in person? He sure went about things in a roundabout way, for someone who seemed to have a lot of confidence in himself.

She peeled off a tiny envelope and opened it. Reaching inside, she found a tiny silver heart-shaped locket on a thin silver chain. "This is beautiful," she gasped, not believing Todd's generosity. She turned the locket over—it was so pretty and delicate. *And so romantic!*

It was way too nice to be left taped to her locker—somebody could easily have taken it. She wondered why Todd had taken such a big risk. She glanced around the hallway to see if he was keeping watch, but she only spotted Aaron, Juan, and a few students she didn't know.

Maybe he got his friends to plant it there, she thought. *He had them watch until I got it.* She smiled and waved at Aaron and Juan, then turned back around to her locker. *Todd's even more wonderful than I thought.* She fastened the tiny locket necklace around her neck. *And he's all mine!*

Elizabeth drummed her fingers against the arm of the living room couch. It was Thursday afternoon, and she was watching a World Cup special, hoping to get some last-minute ideas for the *Sixers*. But Jessica and Robin were so busy talking about the stupid dance that weekend, she couldn't hear the sportscaster say a thing.

"I showed you my new dress when I got here, right?" Robin said.

"It's incredible," Jessica said. "I wish I knew what I was going to wear. Maybe my new blue dress . . . or the one my aunt Helen sent, but I don't know if I have any shoes that go with it."

"Do you guys *mind*?" Elizabeth said. "I'm trying to watch this show."

"Now you know how I feel," Steven commented. He was sitting next to Elizabeth on the couch.

"Sorry," Jessica said. "We didn't know next year's World Cup was more important to you than tomorrow's dance." She and Robin giggled.

"Some of us have more important things on our minds," Elizabeth grumbled.

"Some of us have *minds*," Steven added, and Elizabeth laughed.

"And some of us have dates!" Robin replied pointedly.

Elizabeth glared at her. "And some of us don't run around stealing other people's boyfriends. I don't know how you did it, but I'm never going to forgive you."

"Good," Robin said.

"Fine." Elizabeth turned back to the television.

"Don't tell me the triplets are fighting!" Steven put his hand on his forehead and pretended to faint. "My whole world's fallen apart . . . nothing makes sense anymore . . ."

"Shut up and watch TV," Jessica told him.

"Well, what are you guys fighting about, anyway?" Steven asked Elizabeth. "Is this all about that same boy you—"

"No, it's something else," Jessica interrupted.

"You weren't interested before, so butt out."

"I'm crushed." Steven pressed the volume button on the remote, turning it up several notches.

Elizabeth glanced over at Jessica and Robin. They were still chatting a mile a minute, but to Elizabeth's relief, she couldn't hear what they were saying anymore. How could Robin go on and on about how Todd had agreed to go to the dance with her? She didn't know which was worse: being hurt by Robin, or by Todd.

But she knew one thing very clearly: she wouldn't go to that Sadie Hawkins dance for anything in the world. She hated dances. She hated cousins. And she especially hated boys!

Eleven

"Hi, Juan, this is Jessica. How are you?" Jessica asked on Thursday night.

"Hello, Jessica. I am good, thank you," Juan said.

Jessica felt her heart flutter. *He's so formal. It's totally romantic!*

"So what is up?" Juan asked.

"Oh. You mean, why am I calling?" Jessica said.

"Exactly," Juan said.

Jessica shivered with excitement. Finally. The moment she'd been waiting all week for was here. She leaned back on her bed and put her hand behind her head, holding the cordless phone with her other hand. Robin was in the shower, and she had the place all to herself. "Well, I have a big question to ask you. I was kind of putting it off, because I was afraid . . . well, never mind about *that*."

"What is the question?" Juan wanted to know.

"You know about the dance in the gym tomorrow night, right?" Jessica said. "It's a Sadie Hawkins dance, and that means the girls have to ask the boys. It's an old American custom or something, I guess. There must have been some woman named Sadie Hawkins. Can you imagine having the name Sadie? Wouldn't that be awful?"

"Jessica, what is the question?" Juan repeated. He sounded slightly impatient.

"Oh, right." She was just trying to make conversation, but if Juan wanted her to get to the point, she would. "Well, I was wondering. Would you go to the dance with me?"

Juan coughed. "Uh . . . go to the dance?"

"I know you're probably shocked that I've waited so long to ask you, and it was rude of me, I admit, but—what can I say? I'm a big procrastinator. Ask anyone," Jessica said.

"That's OK." Juan paused. "I mean, I understand."

"You do?" *Of course he does! He's only the most understanding, sweetest, nicest boy on the planet.* Jessica sighed. "So you'll go with me?"

"Well . . . actually . . ."

What? After all her hard work, was he going to say no? "Juan? What's wrong? Don't you want to be my date for the dance?" she asked.

"I don't know," Juan said.

"You don't *know*?" Jessica repeated. What kind of an answer was that?

"You see, I was kind of hoping and expecting that somebody else would ask me," Juan said, sounding nervous.

"Somebody else? Somebody else like *who*?" Jessica demanded.

"This is very embarrassing. It is your cousin, Robin," Juan said. "I am thinking that she might ask me to the dance."

"Well, think again," Jessica muttered. Then she cleared her throat. "What I mean is, I just hate to tell you this, Juan, but she's already going to the dance with someone else. I'm sorry," she added sweetly.

"She's going with someone else?" Juan asked, sounding incredulous. "Are you sure?"

"Call Todd Wilkins yourself if you don't believe me," Jessica said briskly. "Robin asked him today at lunch."

"Today? At lunch? Oh." Juan's voice dropped. "I see."

"Tough break," Jessica said. She hadn't expected Juan to have his heart set on Robin so strongly. What was the big deal about Robin, anyway? OK, so she did have a lot of the same excellent qualities Jessica had, but that should mean they were both irresistible. Jessica had never enjoyed, or even accepted, being someone's second choice before. But, she told herself, some boys, like Juan, were worth sacrificing her pride for. She took a deep breath. "Look, Juan. I know you wanted to go with Robin, but since she's already chosen someone else, my offer still stands."

Jessica crossed her fingers for luck while she waited for Juan's answer. He was silent for a few seconds, and she felt as though she were going to burst with anticipation.

"OK. If you still want me to, I would love to go to the dance with you, Jessica," Juan said.

If I still want you to! "Well, good. I'm really looking forward to it. Thanks!" Jessica said, trying to sound cheerful about being the runner-up.

"No, thank you, Jessica," Juan said. "Now I must go work on my English homework. I will see you tomorrow, yes?"

"Oh, yes," Jessica said, nodding. "You can count on that." She pressed the off button on the phone and laid it beside her on the bed. Then she sank back on the pillow and relaxed. She had her date, and she didn't have to do any more planning, finagling, or impersonating. It was such a relief.

Robin entered the room a few minutes later, wearing a bathrobe, her hair wrapped in a towel. "Well? Did you do it?"

Jessica nodded. "I finally asked him."

"And?"

"He said yes!" Jessica said excitedly. Robin didn't need to know any more than that, not with her date with Todd all lined up.

"We're going to have *so* much fun!" Robin cried. "Maybe the four of us can go together."

"Well, I don't know about *that*," Jessica said. She could just see the four of them sitting at a table, Juan staring at Robin the whole night.

"Why not?" Robin asked.

"Oh, it's just—more romantic when it's only the two of you," Jessica said. "Don't you think?"

"Hmm, that's a good point," Robin said, her eyes sparkling. "I can't wait until tomorrow night!"

"Neither can I," said Jessica. And she *was* excited about tomorrow night—so why did she suddenly feel so sad? She bit her lip. It was really too bad that Elizabeth wouldn't be coming with them. Jessica couldn't think of a single school party she'd been to without her twin.

Elizabeth will get over it, she told herself. *And when she does, she can date whoever she wants to. She'll be so much happier, she'll probably even thank me for fixing up Robin and Todd.*

Anyway, Jessica didn't have time to worry about Elizabeth—she had to decide what she was going to wear to the dance!

"I can't believe you waited until the last minute to ask Juan," Todd overheard Lila say to Jessica on Friday morning. He was standing on the front steps outside school before the homeroom bell rang. Jessica and her friends were just a few feet away.

"You took a big risk," Mandy said. "But you can't argue with the end result. Hey, do you guys want to get together this afternoon and experiment with some makeup?"

"Experiment?" Jessica said. "What do you mean by that?"

Todd turned his attention to the other students gathered on the front steps. *Somebody* had to be talking about something besides the dance that night. So far, everywhere he turned people were talking about what time they were going, what the decorations looked like, what kind of punch would be served—it was driving him crazy!

The more he thought about it, the less he wanted to go with Robin. He didn't know what was going on. First Elizabeth had encouraged him to go with her cousin, even begged him to say yes when Robin asked him. Then, when he did, she got mad at him! He couldn't win. He didn't understand girls. Or at least not Elizabeth—not this time.

He spotted Ken Matthews talking on the sidewalk with Aaron and Juan, and headed down the steps to the three of them. "Hey, you guys, what's up?"

"Hi, Todd. What's going on?" Ken asked.

"I'm so sick of hearing about that dance tonight," Todd complained. "It's all anyone can talk about. I mean, what about the soccer team making the state quarterfinals? Doesn't anyone care about that?"

"I do," Juan said, smiling at him.

"I know," Todd said. "Because you're the one who scored the goals to get us there. But everyone else? Forget about it."

"What's wrong, anyway?" Aaron asked. "Since

when have you complained about spending time with Elizabeth at a dance?"

Todd frowned. "That's just it. I'm not going with Elizabeth."

"What?" Aaron said. "Why not?"

"She has to work on the *Sixers* . . . and so her cousin, Robin, asked me instead," Todd explained.

"Yes, I have heard," Juan said. "Jessica told me." He didn't look too happy.

Aaron frowned. "But I thought you were going with—"

"I am going with Jessica," Juan interrupted.

Aaron went pale. "With Jessica? When did this happen? Why didn't you say something?"

"It is not so important," Juan replied. "Todd is right. Everyone makes too big a deal out of this one little dance."

"But—wait a second," Aaron said. "Weren't you interested in—"

The bell rang, cutting him off. Todd slowly turned and began to trudge inside to homeroom. On his way, he spotted Elizabeth through the crowd. He tried to catch her eye, but when she finally glanced his way, she seemed to look right through him. She didn't say a word.

Todd couldn't stand it any longer. Even though he hadn't meant to, he had obviously hurt Elizabeth's feelings by agreeing to go to the dance with Robin. If he couldn't go with Elizabeth because she was too busy, then he didn't want to go at all.

There was only one thing to do. He had to break his date with Robin, and he had to do it today. He didn't want to upset her, but he *had* to make up with Elizabeth. He'd do whatever it took.

Robin spent her lunch period studying in the school library. She needed to get ready for a quiz that afternoon, and she hadn't gotten any homework done the night before. The library was deserted, and when the door opened, she glanced up from her textbook and saw Todd heading toward her. "Todd! Hi!" she said. "What a nice surprise!" He had actually come to find her, when she hadn't been in the cafeteria. He was so sweet!

"Hi, Robin. Can we talk?" he asked.

"Of course." Robin beamed. Maybe he wanted to ask what kind of corsage to get her for the dance. "What do you want to talk about?"

Todd sat down across from her. "I need to talk to you about tonight. The dance." He fidgeted in his chair. Robin wondered why he seemed so nervous. Didn't they know each other well by now?

"Go ahead," she prompted, her heart beating with anticipation.

"I know you're Elizabeth and Jessica's cousin," Todd began.

What does that have to do with anything? Robin wondered.

"And because of that I've tried to do the right thing, to make everybody happy," he continued, looking down at the tabletop. "I don't want to hurt your feelings—I think you're a really nice person, and you're very pretty, and funny."

"Thanks," Robin said, blushing.

"It's just that . . ." He cleared his throat. "Well, Elizabeth and I have gone to every other school dance together, and I feel really rotten that I'm not going with her—I mean, she is my girlfriend."

"What?" Robin gasped. "Your—girlfriend?"

Todd gave her a confused look. "That's right. She has been for, like, months."

"No, that can't be true," Robin said, shaking her head.

"What are you saying?" Todd asked. "Didn't you know that she and I were—"

"No, I didn't," Robin cut in. "And I don't believe you, Todd. Maybe you have gone on a date with her once or twice, but what about the notes you left in my backpack, on my locker . . . what about the Jujubes you gave me? The silver locket?"

Todd frowned. "I don't know what you're talking about."

"Oh, come on, Todd. I'm not stupid. You sent me all those things, and now you're changing your mind at the last minute? Why? What did Elizabeth do? What did she say about me?" Robin demanded.

"She hasn't done or said anything!" Todd protested. "I don't know anything about Jujubes or a locket or whatever."

"Oh, no?" Robin asked skeptically. "Then who did leave them?"

"I really don't know," Todd said, looking frustrated. "Someone else!"

Robin stared at him. He was so passionate about it, he had to be telling the truth. But that didn't make any sense. If they were boyfriend and girlfriend, why hadn't Elizabeth ever said anything about it to her? And why hadn't Jessica? The whole situation was so confusing, Robin didn't know what to believe. "Are you saying that you and Elizabeth have been dating since before I came to town?" she asked tentatively.

He nodded. "Yeah. I'm sorry, Robin. I just assumed Elizabeth told you."

Robin dropped her eyes. Little by little, she remembered the fight she'd had with Elizabeth a few days before. Elizabeth *had* tried to tell her that she was dating Todd, but Robin hadn't believed her. It just seemed so strange that Elizabeth hadn't mentioned Todd before then and that Todd was being so nice to Robin and— Oh, what was the use? Obviously, Todd and Elizabeth were a couple— Todd said so himself. Robin began shoving her notes into her binder. "Look, I—I have to go," she told Todd. "I'm sorry I made such a huge mistake. You don't have to go to the dance with me tonight—don't worry. I really never meant to come between the two of you—please believe me." She grabbed her binder, stuffed it into her backpack, and headed for the door. She was too humiliated to sit there with Todd another minute.

Robin wiped a tear off her cheek as she hurried down the hall. Now everyone must think she was a total weasel, coming into town and trying to take her cousin's boyfriend. She'd stepped all over Elizabeth—and for what? One little dance? It wasn't worth it. Friendship was much more important. Not to mention cousinhood.

She walked into her next classroom, sighing with relief that it was empty. Class wouldn't start for another few minutes, and she needed to be alone. She spotted a piece of paper lying on her desk. She was about to crumple it and toss it into the recycling basket when she saw her name written in big, neat letters on the outside.

She unfolded the paper. "Dear Robin. I am sorry things did not work out for us. I am sorry if I have been bothering you with my notes and gifts. But I really like you, even if you go to the dance with someone else. Todd is lucky. I wish I could go to the dance with you. Sincerely yours, Juan V."

Robin slid into her seat, completely bewildered. *Juan?* Juan had been the one who gave her the Jujubes and the locket? Juan was her secret admirer? *I should have known!* she thought. *The formal language, the polite gestures—of course it was Juan!*

Robin thought of all the times she had talked to Juan. He was so sweet—nicer than anybody she'd ever met before. She'd thought so the second she met him on Monday. Not only was he polite, he was handsome, and smart, too.

Robin buried her face in her hands. She'd blown everything. She'd hurt Juan's feelings by pursuing Todd. And she'd hurt Elizabeth's feelings by trying to steal Todd from her.

Robin was starting to wish she had never come to Sweet Valley. Some vacation romance! It was turning into a disaster of a vacation instead.

She couldn't wait to get home to San Diego. But first she had to live through one week of humiliation here. She put her head on her desk and sighed. *One very long, horrible week.*

Twelve

◇

At six thirty on Friday night, Elizabeth was sitting at her desk, glaring at the bathroom, which separated her room from Jessica's. She could hear Jessica whistling happily and singing as she got dressed for the dance, and the noise was driving her crazy.

I should be getting ready, too, she thought angrily, tapping her pencil against her desk. *But thanks to Robin and Todd, I'm sitting here pretending to work on the* Sixers *instead.* All she could think about was how, an hour from now, Robin and Todd would be dancing together, while she sat at home, completely miserable.

She wondered what Robin was wearing. What Todd was wearing. Whether he'd bring her a corsage or not. *Stop it!* she tried to tell herself. *You're only making it worse.*

She hadn't talked to Todd since Thursday. A couple of times at school that day, he'd tried to get her attention. But as far as she was concerned, there was nothing to talk about. His accepting a date with her cousin said it all.

"Jessica!" Mrs. Wakefield called up the stairs. "Juan is here!"

"OK, Mom—I'll be right down!" Jessica replied cheerfully.

Elizabeth stared at the bulletin board in front of her desk. On it was a photograph of her and Todd from the last dance they'd been to together. She took out the thumbtack, removed the picture, and shoved it into her middle desk drawer. She had to face facts. She and Todd were history.

She wished she could be happy for Jessica, but she just couldn't. She was too upset.

I hope no one comes looking for me, Robin thought as she flipped through a magazine in the den. She'd heard her aunt Alice call upstairs, and Jessica come running down the stairs, and muffled voices in the living room. Juan and Jessica had to be leaving together any second.

Robin had been hiding out in the den, reading and daydreaming, ever since she got home. She didn't want to talk to Jessica, and she was afraid to talk to Elizabeth. She knew Elizabeth would never believe her side of the story, that she hadn't known about her and Todd. And she didn't trust Jessica, after what had happened. Jessica should have told her about Todd and Elizabeth—but instead she encouraged her to go after Todd! Maybe she was just trying to be a good friend, but she hadn't considered Elizabeth's feelings at all.

The front door closed. Robin went to the window and cautiously peered out. She saw Juan wearing a dark suit—probably black. *That would look great with my dress*, she thought, dejected. Jessica was wearing a coat over her outfit, so Robin couldn't see it. *But I'm sure it's totally beautiful*. Juan opened the back door of Lila's father's limousine, and guided Jessica inside. *That should be me*.

When she'd told Jessica she wouldn't be going to the dance, Jessica had been shocked. Robin hadn't wanted to tell her the real reason, so she'd made up a story about Todd not feeling well. As the limo pulled out into the street, Robin sighed and leaned back on the love seat. As bad as she was feeling, she knew that Elizabeth was hibernating upstairs in her room, feeling ten times worse.

And it's all my fault, Robin thought miserably. Then she got an idea. Maybe she couldn't do anything to make Elizabeth feel better, but she knew someone who probably could. She wouldn't believe it if Robin told her what happened, but she'd have to believe Todd . . . wouldn't she?

Robin grabbed the phone book off her uncle Ned's desk and flipped through it until she found the listing for Wilkins. Nervously, she punched the number on the keypad. "Hello, Todd? This is Robin," she said when Todd answered the phone.

"Hi, Robin," Todd said, sounding a little uncomfortable.

"I don't mean to bug you, but Elizabeth's really bummed," Robin said. "She's trying to get that special edition of the paper done, but . . . she needs help."

"Really?" Todd asked.

"Yeah. So I thought, since I knew you were at home and you probably want to see Elizabeth . . . maybe you could come over and tell her you'll help her," Robin said.

"Robin? Do you think there's any chance she'll talk to me?" Todd asked. "I tried to explain today, but—"

"I know. She doesn't want to talk to me, either," Robin said quickly. "But I think she'll listen to you, Todd. All you can do is try, right?"

"I'll be over as fast as I can get there," Todd promised. "Thanks, Robin."

"Sure thing." Robin hung up the phone. She hoped Elizabeth was in a forgiving mood. She was supposed to stay in Elizabeth's room all next week, and she didn't want to miss out on that.

Besides, she couldn't hide out in the den forever. She was running out of things to read!

Elizabeth had finally stopped moping and was just starting to proofread the front page of the *Sixers* when there was a knock on her door.

"Elizabeth?" Robin said softly.

"Go away," Elizabeth said, frowning. "I'm working. And I don't want to talk to you."

"But there's someone here to see you," Robin protested.

Who? Elizabeth wondered. Then it hit her. Todd had come over to pick up Robin, and they wanted to throw it in her face. *Of all the nerve!* "I hope you're not expecting me to wish you and Todd well on your date. You won the war—fine. But don't rub it in!"

"No, Elizabeth. Todd's not here for me. We're not going to the dance—haven't you noticed? It's already eight o'clock," Robin said.

Elizabeth glanced at her clock. Robin was right. If they were going to the dance, they were pretty late. But Elizabeth stayed seated at her desk. "And?" she asked.

"And Todd's here to see *you*," Robin said.

"Really?" Elizabeth felt a little flutter of excitement despite herself.

"Yes, really. So are you going to come downstairs or not? He's waiting," Robin said.

Elizabeth opened the door. "Are you going to be there, too?" she asked sternly.

"Only at first—I need to explain something," Robin said. "Then I'll take off and leave you guys alone. I promise."

"Well . . . OK." Elizabeth followed her down the stairs and into the kitchen.

Todd was sitting at the kitchen table. He stood up when they walked into the room. "Hi, Elizabeth.

Here, this is for you. I don't know if it matches your robe, but . . ." He held out a single red rose.

Elizabeth stared at the rose. "One little rose doesn't make up for anything."

Todd held it out to her. "I know, but it's a start, isn't it?" he asked, sounding truly upset.

"That depends," Elizabeth said.

"Come on, Elizabeth. *Please* accept it. I'm sorry," Todd said.

"Well . . . OK. Thanks." Elizabeth finally took the rose from him.

"It even matches your bathrobe," Todd said with a faint smile.

Elizabeth glanced down at her red flannel robe and blushed. *Why didn't you change first?* she scolded herself.

"And before you can say anything else, please let me explain something," Todd said. "I only asked Robin to the dance because you told me to. I never wanted to go with anyone besides you. But you told me—"

"What? I never told you to ask her," Elizabeth said.

"Yes, you did. That day in the library," Todd said. "You said that you were going to be busy working on the paper, and that since Robin had been turned down by some other guy, it would be really nice if I agreed to go with her, and that's the only reason I said yes when she asked me."

"Todd, are you making this up?" Elizabeth

asked. "Maybe you had a *dream* that's what I said, but I never said anything like that."

"It had to be a dream, because for one thing, I never asked anyone else to the dance!" Robin added. "So I don't know why Elizabeth would have said that—it wasn't true."

"But I don't get it," Todd said.

"Before you guys say anything else, Elizabeth, I found out something today, and you have to believe me on this," Robin pleaded. "I honestly never knew that you and Todd were already a couple."

"What? But that's impossible," Elizabeth said. "I'm sure I told you before—on the phone, in a letter . . ."

"No, you never did," Robin said. "And Jessica never did, either. So when I met Todd and I told her I liked him, she told me he was available and—"

"Wait a second," Elizabeth said. "Jessica said what?"

"When I told her I liked Todd, I asked if he was, you know, dating anyone." Robin glanced nervously at Todd, who looked equally embarrassed. "And she said no, so I just figured—"

"Jessica told you that Todd was available, so you decided to ask him to the dance," Elizabeth finished.

"Right," Robin said.

Elizabeth frowned. Why would Jessica lie to Robin about her and Todd? *Why would she do that?* Elizabeth wondered.

"I'm really sorry I didn't believe you when you tried to tell me about you and Todd after I saw you guys at Casey's," Robin continued. "I was just so sure Todd was my secret admirer." She blushed. "Then I found out today who it really was—it was Juan."

"Juan," Elizabeth repeated, her mind whirling. It was all starting to come together. Juan liked Robin, and Jessica liked Juan. The only way to get Robin out of the picture was for Robin to have a date with someone else. Todd. So she'd impersonated Elizabeth, turned Todd over to Robin, and now she was at the dance with Juan, just as she wanted. "Jessica's been pretty busy," she said.

"What do you mean?" Robin asked.

"Todd, I never told you to ask Robin to the dance," Elizabeth explained. "That was Jessica, pretending to be me!"

"But why?" Robin said.

Elizabeth quickly explained the sequence of events she had just figured out. "And *that's* what she was up to."

"Pretty sneaky, even for Jessica," Todd commented.

"I'll say," Steven said.

Elizabeth turned around and saw him standing behind her in the doorway. She'd been so busy talking that she hadn't even heard him come in.

"She even came to me to ask me what to do, but did she take my advice?" Steven asked, shaking his head vigorously. "Well, she kind of did, but I never told her to pull a stunt like this. Now she's at the dance with the guy *you're* supposed to be with," he said to Robin. "Some hostess."

"She's having fun, and we're stuck at home," Robin complained. "It's not fair."

"You're right, it's not," Elizabeth said. "And you know what else? I have an idea of how we can get back at her—tonight."

"How?" Todd asked.

"I'll explain in the car. Hey, Mom!" Elizabeth called into the living room. "Can you give us a ride to school?"

Mrs. Wakefield came into the kitchen, looking confused. "Do you mean you're going to the dance after all?" She stared at Elizabeth's robe.

Elizabeth nodded. "And it's going to be a night to remember!"

Thirteen

"I wonder what Jessica was wearing," Elizabeth said as she and Robin ran upstairs to get dressed. "Do you have any idea?"

"I was watching out the window, but it was pretty dark and she had a coat on," Robin said, walking into Jessica's bedroom, where her dress was hanging in the closet. "I think she was planning on a red dress, but I'm not really sure. Why?"

"The only way to get her back is do the same kind of thing she did to us," Elizabeth explained. "And that means I have to impersonate her."

Steven knocked on the side of the door. "Did you say something about impersonating?"

"Yeah, why?" Elizabeth asked.

"Because I happen to know exactly what Jessica was wearing tonight," Steven said calmly. He pulled a Polaroid photo out of his back pocket. "She made me take her and Juan's picture about ten times before she left. This is one of the rejects." He handed it to Elizabeth.

"This is perfect!" Elizabeth cried. "She's wearing a dress that Aunt Helen bought for *both* of us. At the time, I thought we wouldn't be caught dead wearing the same dress, but it's going to come in *very* handy tonight. Thanks, Steven!"

"No problem," he said. "Hey, Todd, come to my room—I can lend you a jacket. You don't want to look like a total slouch."

Todd and Steven headed down the hallway, and Elizabeth just stood in the doorway, gazing after them. She and Todd were back together. Everything was going to work out. She grabbed the pale-green dress from her closet, then ran back to Jessica's room and closed the door so they could get changed.

"What's gotten into Steven?" Robin asked, slipping her long, cranberry-colored dress over her head. "He's being pretty helpful, considering how rude we've been to him."

"We have been rude," Elizabeth conceded. "But Jessica's been the rudest, and Steven never misses a chance to get her. He's going to love what happens tonight."

"Not as much as I am!" Robin said, and she and Elizabeth laughed.

*   *   *

Todd, Elizabeth, and Robin rushed into the gym. "Oh, no—it's practically over!" Robin pointed to the clock on the wall. It was ten minutes to nine.

"Don't worry—we have enough time," Elizabeth said. She scanned the crowd, looking for Juan and Jessica. The gym was nicely decorated, with streamers hanging from the ceiling. The place was packed with almost everyone she knew from school.

"And now, the moment you've all been waiting for . . ." the disc jockey announced dramatically. "The final dance of the evening . . . our sweethearts dance. Everyone find your partner and . . . wait a second here. I can't quite find the CD I need." He glanced nervously at the crowd, then ducked under the table and started rifling through his CD collection.

"There they are!" Todd said, pointing to the side of the gym where the refreshment table had been set up. Juan and Jessica were standing together, next to several of Jessica's friends and their dates.

"I think Jessica's going to get some punch or something—here's your chance," Robin said eagerly.

Elizabeth fluffed out her hair around her shoulders and reapplied a fresh coat of the pink lip gloss Jessica always wore. "Wish me luck."

"We'll hide over here in the shadows," Robin said. "You're going to do great."

"Good luck . . . Jessica," Todd said, squeezing her arm.

Elizabeth smiled, and when Jessica turned her back to pour herself a cup of punch and talk to Lila, she walked right over to Juan, putting on her best Jessica saunter. "Juan, I've been having a *great* time," she said.

He looked at Elizabeth. "I thought you wanted something to drink."

"Oh, I do," Elizabeth said. "But I was halfway there when I realized there was something I just had to tell you first." She smiled at him and batted her eyelashes. Juan looked nervous. *He probably thinks I'm going to tell him I'm in love with him!* Elizabeth thought, trying her hardest not to laugh.

"What is it?" Juan asked.

"Well," she began, then paused dramatically. "Even though I think you're wonderful—really the most wonderful person in the world—I know that you don't feel the same way about me."

"I don't?" Juan said.

"No." She looked at him meaningfully. "I know I'm not the girl you really wanted to go to the dance with. And there's no way I'd ever stand in the way of true love. I believe in fate one hundred percent. That's why I feel like I have to tell you that the girl who really likes you and belongs with you is my cousin, Robin."

Juan's eyes lit up.

"She's standing right over there, by the door," Elizabeth continued. "I know I've hogged the whole evening, but you guys still have time for one dance. Why don't you ask her to dance the last dance?"

Elizabeth had barely finished the sentence when

Juan took off like a shot. "Thanks, Jessica!" he called over his shoulder. Within seconds, he had rushed over to Robin, who had stepped out of the shadow just as the first notes for the sweetheart dance trickled out of the large speakers.

Elizabeth smiled as she watched them look shyly at each other. Then Juan put his arms around Robin's waist and guided her onto the dance floor.

Maybe Jessica's onto something, she thought. *This playing matchmaker is kind of rewarding.*

"So, Jessica, what do you say? Would you like to dance?"

Elizabeth turned around and saw Todd standing behind her. "OK, but I think I was supposed to ask you first."

Todd grinned. "You're right. In fact, we never would have so many problems if you'd just asked me to the dance right away, like you should have!"

"Well, excuse me," Elizabeth said, flipping her hair over her shoulder the way Jessica always did. "But some of us just assume everyone will want to go with us."

Todd put his arms around her waist. "Actually, the person I wanted to dance with was Elizabeth. Is she around anywhere?"

"Oh . . . I think I can find her," Elizabeth said, putting her hands on Todd's shoulders as they moved into the crowd. She and Todd slowly danced their way over to Robin and Juan, and when she caught Robin's eye, Elizabeth gave her the thumbs-up signal. Robin smiled at her and waved. Juan turned around to see who she was waving at. At the sight of Todd dancing with Jessica, he looked completely confused.

Elizabeth laughed. *If that's his reaction, wait until Jessica sees the four of us!*

Jessica couldn't believe it. The last dance of the night, and Juan was nowhere to be found? She'd been standing in the same spot for an entire minute, waiting for him to come back from the bathroom or wherever he was. No sign of him anywhere.

She chewed the lip of the empty plastic punch cup in her hand. If she and Juan didn't dance the sweetheart dance together, it meant two very bad things: one, he didn't really like her, and two, everyone else would know he didn't! She couldn't stand that kind of humiliation, not at one of the biggest dances of the year. Not ever, for that matter, she reflected unhappily.

Everyone was on the dance floor but her and a bunch of nerds who didn't have dates. Including Aaron, who was standing beside her at the refreshment table. He kept staring at her. *He's probably getting ready to gloat,* she thought.

All of a sudden she saw a flash of green—the same color green her dress was. *Don't tell me someone else has the same dress!* she thought. Things were going from bad to worse. Talk about public humiliation!

Then she saw who was wearing the dress. Elizabeth! And she was dancing with Todd! But wait a second—that didn't make any sense. Where was Robin?

She stood on her tiptoes and glanced around the gym. She was focusing on Lila and Jake when Juan and Robin waltzed right past her. She stared at them as they disappeared into the crowd. *What? Juan and Robin? How did that happen?*

If Juan and Robin were together, and Todd and Elizabeth were back together, and Elizabeth was wearing the same dress . . . What was going on? Jessica felt as if she were stuck on a math word problem . . . a *bad* word problem.

Then it hit her. The only reason Elizabeth would dress just like Jessica was if she wanted everyone to think she *was* Jessica. Or not everyone, exactly—just Juan. Jessica stood on the edge of the dance floor, frozen in shock. Elizabeth had somehow managed to get back together with Todd, and to hand Juan over to Robin. All while Jessica had turned around for two seconds because she was thirsty!

"I never should have had that second cup," she muttered, tossing her empty cup into the trash.

Elizabeth and Todd and Robin and Juan came back into view. Elizabeth took a few steps away from Todd and smiled at Jessica. "You're not the only Wakefield who can play matchmaker!" she said triumphantly. Then she kept dancing.

"Oh, hi, Jessica!" Robin exclaimed just before

Juan swept her out into the middle of the dance floor and twirled her in a circle.

Jessica glared at the two of them. Life just wasn't fair. She wished she'd never even shown up at this stupid Sadie Hawkins Dance! Betrayed by her own sister, taunted by her very own cousin—really, it was a bit much.

Aaron took a step closer to Jessica. "Don't you just hate houseguests?" he asked, frowning at Juan.

"With a passion," Jessica agreed, watching Robin laugh as Juan spun her around on the dance floor and lowered her in a dramatic dip.

"Still, Juan is a great guy. He fits in really well here, don't you think?" Aaron asked. "Almost like he should move here."

"I don't know about that," Jessica said, narrowing her eyes as the kids around Robin and Juan stepped back to watch and applaud.

"And his English is getting better every day," Aaron went on. "Even if he sometimes needs help, like when he's shopping for presents for American girls, or writing love notes."

Jessica turned and stared at Aaron. He was grinning. "You actually *helped* him? You knew he liked Robin, and you helped him—when you knew I liked him?"

Aaron shrugged. "Sorry, Jessica. But you know what they say. 'All's fair in love and war.'"

I've heard, Jessica thought angrily. *But I don't see what's fair about any of this!*

"And I just couldn't stand there and watch you go to the dance with another guy," Aaron said softly.

Jessica met Aaron's eyes. She didn't know whether she wanted to punch him or hug him. If he hadn't helped and encouraged Juan to pursue Robin, Juan might have given up, changed his mind, and fallen for Jessica. Then again, Aaron did seem to be pining after her. Maybe he even adored her—and adoration won points, in Jessica's book. OK, so he didn't have a foreign accent, and maybe sometimes it was fun to go on dates with other people. But he was still one of the best-looking boys in the sixth grade, and he was nice besides.

She smiled at him. "You know what? You're cute when you're jealous. Let's dance."

Aaron smiled and took her hand.

Maybe the night wouldn't be a disaster after all.

Fourteen

◇

"I know I already apologized, but I really am sorry," Jessica said, taking a seat on the carpet in Elizabeth's room.

Robin grinned. "Really? *How* sorry?" she teased. "Like, I know you already brought me and Elizabeth apples, but would you go down to the kitchen and get that tin of oatmeal raisin cookies?"

It was about ten thirty, and Jessica, Elizabeth, and Robin had all gathered in Elizabeth's room to rehash the dance. It was the first time the three of them had been together—and not fighting—in a few days, so they had a lot of catching up to do.

"Please. I might be sorry, but I'm not stupid," Jessica said, settling back against the bed.

"Oh, come on, Jessica—I think it's the *least* you could do, considering," Elizabeth said, brushing her hair. "I mean, what if Juan somehow happened to find out that you . . ."

"All right, already," Jessica grumbled, getting to her feet. "But that's it! What I did wasn't *so* horrible."

Robin and Elizabeth laughed as Jessica ran downstairs. She came back a minute later and placed the tin on the floor, along with three sodas. "In case we get thirsty," she said, smiling at both of them.

"Gee, thanks, Jessica," Elizabeth said, sitting down beside her. "A couple more favors like this and we might just forgive you."

"What's to forgive? Didn't you have a good time at the dance?" Jessica asked her.

"Definitely," Elizabeth sighed.

"And didn't you?" Jessica asked Robin, who beamed and nodded. "Well, then. I rest my case," Jessica said.

"I'm so glad Mr. Clark decided to let the dance go another half hour," Robin said, cracking open a soda. She leaned back against the pillows on Elizabeth's bed. She'd changed out of her fancy dress and into her flannel pajamas—she felt totally comfortable. "It would have been awful if we had to leave at nine."

"No kidding," Elizabeth said, kicking off her shoes. She reached into her desk drawer, pulled out a picture of her and Todd, and pinned it on her bulletin board. "Especially since we'd barely just gotten there. Thanks to yours truly." She pointed an accusing finger at Jessica.

"I can't keep apologizing," Jessica protested.

"It's getting boring. Anyway, it's not like you guys didn't ruin *my* night, too."

"*We* ruined *your* night?" Elizabeth scoffed. "Gee, we're so sorry, aren't we, Robin? Little Miss Matchmaker here didn't have a good time." She gave Jessica a playful nudge with her toe.

"Well, at least it wasn't a *total* loss," Jessica said. "I did get to see you guys having fun." She smiled faintly. "You and Juan looked cute together."

"So did you and Todd," Robin told Elizabeth. "I can see why you guys get along so well, too. He's a great guy."

"A little on the dull side, but—" Jessica began. Elizabeth folded her arms and glared at her. "But sometimes dull is good. Dull in an . . . interesting way."

Elizabeth laughed. "So did you have fun with Aaron? I saw you guys dancing. Who was he there with, anyway?"

"Nobody," Jessica said. "He said he didn't want to go with anyone besides me."

"How romantic!" Robin cried.

"Kind of," Jessica said, blushing. "Actually, yeah. We were having a great time dancing." Then she frowned. "That is, until Bruce got out his dumb Watchman and Aaron ran over to check out the score of the Lakers game."

"So did Todd," Elizabeth complained. "Only, he didn't just check the score—he watched the last ten minutes of the game."

"So did Juan," Robin added. Bruce Patman had brought his portable television to the dance, and as soon as he turned it on and tuned in the basketball playoffs, all the guys had taken off to watch the game. Robin didn't really mind, except that she would have liked to have a few more dances with Juan.

"Did you see them? They were acting like that game was a matter of life or death," Jessica said. "As if a basketball game could be more interesting and exciting than *me*."

Robin shook her head. "Sometimes I don't understand boys at all."

"To friends," Jessica said, holding up her can of soda. "The only people worth counting on."

The girls clinked their soda cans.

"And to cousins," Robin added. "Thanks for a great time!"

"It's not over yet," Elizabeth said. "You still have a week to spend with us—and with Juan."

"I know," Robin said dreamily. She turned to Jessica. "You're not mad at me, are you? I mean, because Juan likes me?"

"You mean, because he picked you when he could have had the one and only Jessica Wakefield?" Jessica asked. "Well . . . if it had to happen, I'm glad we at least kept it in the family."

"Doesn't that ever happen with you guys?" Robin asked. "It must all the time. You like someone, Elizabeth, only he likes Jessica, and vice versa?"

"Actually, it's really easy, because everyone always

likes me—and Elizabeth isn't interested in anyone but Todd!" Jessica declared with a smile.

"Oh, is that so?" Elizabeth asked. "Nobody's ever liked *me* first?"

Jessica pretended to study her nails. "Not that I can remember."

"Liar!" Elizabeth said, tossing a pillow at her twin.

"Give me one good example!" Jessica replied, throwing it back in Elizabeth's face.

"I could give you a hundred examples," Elizabeth said, "only we don't have all night!"

"Yes we do!" Robin said. "And I want to hear it all!" She picked up a pillow and hit Jessica over the head.

Soon, the room was a flurry of pillows, and Elizabeth, Robin, and Jessica were shrieking at the top of their lungs about who liked who first, and why.

"He did not!" Jessica cried.

"He did too!" Elizabeth replied, bashing her sister in the nose with a down pillow.

"Well, that's only because I was *busy* that night!" Jessica said.

"Yeah, right!" Robin said, and Jessica tackled her. Robin screamed.

There was a loud banging on the door, and all three girls sat up. Robin put her hand over her mouth. They were really in trouble this time.

"C-come in," Elizabeth panted.

Robin held her breath. Steven opened the door and walked into the room.

"Don't say it—we know," Jessica said. "We'll stop."

"No, you won't," Steven said. "But that's OK. I've thought it over, and I've decided something."

"You're renting an apartment?" Robin asked.

"Nope." Steven sat down on the floor next to her. "You know what they say: If you can't beat 'em, join 'em. So what were you guys yelling about?"

"Steven, did we *invite* you in here?" Jessica asked.

Steven looked at her with a hurt expression. "Well, no, but—"

"What makes you think you can just waltz in here and listen to our deepest, most intimate secrets?" Elizabeth said.

Steven shrugged. "Sorry, I just thought—"

"Well, you thought wrong. Not just anyone can join this club," Robin said.

Steven looked genuinely upset. "Hey, give me a break. I was only trying to be nice." He stood up and was about to leave the room when the three girls burst out laughing.

"I couldn't hold it in any longer!" Elizabeth exclaimed.

"I can't believe he fell for it!" Robin cried.

"Steven, sit down already and have a cookie," Jessica said. "Did you expect a printed invitation or something?"

Steven just shook his head as he joined their circle on the floor and took a cookie out of the tin. "Girls."

"So, Steven. Want to know your horoscope?" Robin asked. "Jessica's really good at them." She tossed a magazine to her cousin and smiled. She was so glad that they were all friends again. Her cousins were the best in the world.

Even Steven.

"I'm so bummed that Robin's gone," Jessica said to Elizabeth at Casey's on a Sunday afternoon a week after the dance. Robin had just left for San Diego that morning. "I personally think she should move to Sweet Valley."

Elizabeth laughed. "That would be fun. I'm just not so sure her parents would be thrilled with that idea."

"Well, maybe we can visit her soon," Jessica mused.

Elizabeth nodded. "I hope so. But in the meantime, I can't wait for that field trip next week." The twins and their classmates were taking a ferry to a Pacific island known for its beautiful wildlife—porpoises and unusual birds.

Jessica's face lit up. "It'll be like a cruise almost! I bet I'll get a great tan!"

"You're probably right, but that's not *all* there is to the trip, you know," Elizabeth said, smiling. "I'm sure it'll be a great adventure."

What's in store for the twins on their field trip to the island? Find out in Sweet Valley Twins #91, Deadly Voyage.

Bantam Books in the SWEET VALLEY TWINS series.
Ask your bookseller for the books you have missed.

#1 BEST FRIENDS
#2 TEACHER'S PET
#3 THE HAUNTED HOUSE
#4 CHOOSING SIDES
#5 SNEAKING OUT
#6 THE NEW GIRL
#7 THREE'S A CROWD
#8 FIRST PLACE
#9 AGAINST THE RULES
#10 ONE OF THE GANG
#11 BURIED TREASURE
#12 KEEPING SECRETS
#13 STRETCHING THE TRUTH
#14 TUG OF WAR
#15 THE OLDER BOY
#16 SECOND BEST
#17 BOYS AGAINST GIRLS
#18 CENTER OF ATTENTION
#19 THE BULLY
#20 PLAYING HOOKY
#21 LEFT BEHIND
#22 OUT OF PLACE

#23 CLAIM TO FAME
#24 JUMPING TO CONCLUSIONS
#25 STANDING OUT
#26 TAKING CHARGE
#27 TEAMWORK
#28 APRIL FOOL!
#29 JESSICA AND THE BRAT ATTACK
#30 PRINCESS ELIZABETH
#31 JESSICA'S BAD IDEA
#32 JESSICA ON STAGE
#33 ELIZABETH'S NEW HERO
#34 JESSICA, THE ROCK STAR
#35 AMY'S PEN PAL
#36 MARY IS MISSING
#37 THE WAR BETWEEN THE TWINS
#38 LOIS STRIKES BACK
#39 JESSICA AND THE MONEY MIX-UP
#40 DANNY MEANS TROUBLE
#41 THE TWINS GET CAUGHT
#42 JESSICA'S SECRET
#43 ELIZABETH'S FIRST KISS
#44 AMY MOVES IN

Sweet Valley Twins Super Editions
#1 THE CLASS TRIP
#2 HOLIDAY MISCHIEF

#3 THE BIG CAMP SECRET
#4 THE UNICORNS GO HAWAIIAN
#5 LILA'S SECRET VALENTINE

Sweet Valley Twins Super Chiller Editions
#1 THE CHRISTMAS GHOST
#2 THE GHOST IN THE GRAVEYARD
#3 THE CARNIVAL GHOST
#4 THE GHOST IN THE BELL TOWER

#5 THE CURSE OF THE RUBY NECKLACE
#6 THE CURSE OF THE GOLDEN HEART
#7 THE HAUNTED BURIAL GROUND
#8 THE SECRET OF THE MAGIC PEN

Sweet Valley Twins Magna Editions
THE MAGIC CHRISTMAS
BIG FOR CHRISTMAS

A CHRISTMAS WITHOUT ELIZABETH

#45 LUCY TAKES THE REINS
#46 MADEMOISELLE JESSICA
#47 JESSICA'S NEW LOOK
#48 MANDY MILLER FIGHTS BACK
#49 THE TWINS' LITTLE SISTER
#50 JESSICA AND THE SECRET STAR
#51 ELIZABETH THE IMPOSSIBLE
#52 BOOSTER BOYCOTT
#53 THE SLIME THAT ATE SWEET VALLEY
#54 THE BIG PARTY WEEKEND
#55 BROOKE AND HER ROCK-STAR MOM
#56 THE WAKEFIELDS STRIKE IT RICH
#57 BIG BROTHER'S IN LOVE!
#58 ELIZABETH AND THE ORPHANS
#59 BARNYARD BATTLE
#60 CIAO, SWEET VALLEY!
#61 JESSICA THE NERD
#62 SARAH'S DAD AND SOPHIA'S MOM
#63 POOR LILA!
#64 THE CHARM SCHOOL MYSTERY
#65 PATTY'S LAST DANCE
#66 THE GREAT BOYFRIEND SWITCH

#67 JESSICA THE THIEF
#68 THE MIDDLE SCHOOL GETS MARRIED
#69 WON'T SOMEONE HELP ANNA?
#70 PSYCHIC SISTERS
#71 JESSICA SAVES THE TREES
#72 THE LOVE POTION
#73 LILA'S MUSIC VIDEO
#74 ELIZABETH THE HERO
#75 JESSICA AND THE EARTHQUAKE
#76 YOURS FOR A DAY
#77 TODD RUNS AWAY
#78 STEVEN THE ZOMBIE
#79 JESSICA'S BLIND DATE
#80 THE GOSSIP WAR
#81 ROBBERY AT THE MALL
#82 STEVEN'S ENEMY
#83 AMY'S SECRET SISTER
#84 ROMEO AND 2 JULIETS
#85 ELIZABETH THE SEVENTH-GRADER
#86 IT CAN'T HAPPEN HERE
#87 THE MOTHER-DAUGHTER SWITCH
#88 STEVEN GETS EVEN
#89 JESSICA'S COOKIE DISASTER
#90 THE COUSIN WAR

SIGN
SWE
FAN

Hey, gi
Valley
when y
As a m
cool st

- Men
  pers
- A Sw
  Treas
- Swe
- Offic
  note
- Three
- A "M
- Two
  Floss
  leafle
- Two
- Plus
  prod
  conte

Be the
Sweet
for U.S
& hand
Send a
High®
SWEET

NAME

ADDRE

CITY

AGE
Offer go
codes o
©1993 b

28 Days

DATE DUE			
MAR 1 8 2000			

PBj

The cousin war